THE
BLESSING

THE HEWEY CALLOWAY NOVELS

By Elmer Kelton

The Smiling Country

The Good Old Boys

Six Bits a Day

By Steve Kelton

The Unlikely Lawman

By Steve Kelton and John Bradshaw

The Familiar Stranger

By John Bradshaw

The Blessing

Elmer Kelton's

THE
BLESSING

A Hewey Calloway
Adventure

John Bradshaw

DEVIL'S CLAW PRESS

Paperback ISBN: 979-8-9939675-0-9

To Boone, my son.

Chapter One

1913

Hewey Calloway eased the red roan colt to a stop a few hundred yards from the Circle W headquarters, the setting sun casting long shadows on the rocky ground before them. Twenty miles to the east, the Del Norte Mountains rose above the arid Trans Pecos country south of Alpine, and not far to the north stood the smaller Puertecita Mountains. The Circle W Ranch Hewey had been running for the past few years stretched a good distance toward each range. A man could make some horse tracks and never leave the place.

A few scattered wood and rock buildings and corrals made up the headquarters in the flat below. There was not much to it, but it had been home for the last three years, and three years was a long time for Hewey Calloway to stay tied to one place.

Hewey could not have said exactly how old he was, because he was not completely certain of the year he had been born. He knew he had passed forty, and that had been two or three years earlier. That was a close enough estimation for him. The years had finally put a little weight on him. He was still thin, just no longer skinny.

Among the plain buildings below him was a small rock house where he and Spring had lived since coming to the ranch a week after their wedding three years earlier. The house was a benefit of being the ranch foreman. Hewey still mostly disliked the responsibility that came with his position, but he grudgingly and quietly appreciated the comforts and privacy the house afforded him and Spring.

Another thought he had never voiced aloud was the sense of pride he felt that he had managed the sprawling Circle W for these past years, and that the ranch had done quite well under his supervision. They had slowly improved the quality of the cattle. A crew running a mule-drawn grader had built several dirt tanks to catch the runoff that flowed after the infrequent West Texas rains, which allowed the cattle to make better use of certain portions of the ranch that had been too far from drinking water beforehand. The fruits of their many labors were beginning to be seen.

The ranch had been profitable. Hewey knew this not from any sort of comment or compliment from Old Man Morgan Jenkins, the ranch's owner, but rather from the lack of complaint. Jenkins was as stingy with kind words as he was with his dollars, and in his case that meant something.

There was movement in one of the corrals below, and Hewey could hear hooves pounding the hard ground inside. A horse squealed and a man grunted. The corral sides were solid, made of slim, vertical mesquite posts, so Hewey could not see what was happening inside.

Probably Enrique, Hewey thought to himself. Enrique was Aparicio Rodriguez's nephew, a slender youth not long out of Mexico who had an easy smile, no matter the circumstance. He had been quiet when he first arrived at the ranch, but he had slowly grown comfortable and talkative. He was all the horseman of his uncle and perhaps a touch more.

According to Aparicio, this skill with horses was due to their roots near Ojinaga, Chihuahua, which was just across the border from Presidio, about fifty miles southwest of the ranch. The best caballeros came from just outside Ojinaga, Aparicio had told Hewey one morning as they trotted side by side through the ranch. It was in their sangre, their blood.

While most of the older hands were content to relax for an hour or two in the evening when the regular work was done, Enrique was usually found at the corral working with one of the younger horses. He enjoyed it, and there just was not much else to do for an energetic youth in such a remote area when the daylight stretched so far into the evening.

Hewey and the roan were easing toward the corral to satisfy his curiosity when he was diverted from course by a child's laughter. A hundred feet from the main house stood another rock house, similar in style yet smaller in size. These had originally been built to house the owner and the foreman, but since Morgan

Jenkins lived in Alpine, Hewey and Spring took the "big" house. As the only family man on the crew, Aparicio Rodriguez was given the foreman's house. There might have been a touch of resentment among a couple of the white cowboys over a Mexican hand getting a house while they lived in the bunkhouse, but none had been foolish enough to voice their discontent to Hewey.

Between the two old houses was an open area, a yard of sorts, although the grass was limited to a few wispy clumps here and there. Hewey turned the corner of the big house to see Aparicio, on foot for a change, slowly leading Hewey's aging brown horse, Biscuit, in a large circle. Proudly perched bareback astride the horse was Elena, Aparicio's two-year-old daughter, hanging on tightly to Biscuit's mane.

Sitting in the shade on the porch of the smaller house watching was Spring, and next to her was Aparicio's wife, Olivia.

The roan colt was tired and happy to stand quietly. Hewey sat in silence, taking in the scene. It made him happy to watch Elena, a beautiful little girl who had been born next door and who was very much like a niece to him and Spring. But it also caused a pain in his chest, a longing that he had never known could exist, not until recent years.

Pushing aside those thoughts, Hewey grinned at his friend. "She's lookin' good," Hewey said. "She'll have your job before you know it."

The Blessing

Aparicio beamed with pride. "I told you, my friend. It is in the blood. You have a little Ojinaga in you, you're gon' be a good caballero." He looked up at his delighted daughter. "Or caballera."

Hewey rode over to the porch and stopped the roan with a gentle pull on the mecate. The roan was only three years old and still in a hackamore. Hewey might have been forced to give up riding the roughest broncs, but he had healed enough since that black stud nearly killed him several years earlier that he was no longer stuck riding Biscuit and a few of the older, gentler horses. He kept a few young horses in his string. He let Aparicio or Enrique ride them a month or two, then he took over.

Olivia Rodriguez looked up at him and smiled, her teeth white against her brown skin. She was a pretty woman of about twenty-five, short and not as slim as she once was, but she was unendingly cheerful. She and Spring had become great friends despite such drastically different backgrounds.

"Buenas noches, patron," Olivia said. She always called him patron, simply because she knew it aggravated him.

Hewey tried to look disapproving but failed. Olivia saw through it and laughed aloud. Elena may have been born with her father's natural ability with a horse, but the little girl got her mother's personality.

Spring said, "I saved you some supper. You weren't back so we went ahead, but it's still warm."

Spring was looking at him, a pained smile on her face. Hewey forced a grin, trying to cheer his wife. He knew well what was going on in her mind. He could read it plain as day every time Spring looked at little Elena.

"Let me unsaddle this pony, then I'll be right back," he said. Hewey and Aparicio typically ate breakfast with the cowboys, since they left so early in the morning to escape some of the heat. But both men tried to eat with their families as much as possible.

Aparicio pulled Elena off Biscuit's back and turned the brown horse loose where he stood. Biscuit had the run of the place. He never strayed too far, and he would amble up to headquarters anytime someone whistled at him, hoping for a few oats.

Hewey watched Biscuit slowly ease toward a small patch of green grass just off the porch where Olivia dumped her dishwater. The aging gelding was fat and lazy. Hewey smiled to himself, then said quietly, "Derned old pensioner."

The next morning, Hewey had almost reached the barn when the first rooster crowed, and this particular skinny white rooster was an early riser. There was a faint glow showing above the mountains far to the east, but sunrise was still a good hour away.

Spring and Olivia had insisted on acquiring the chickens a couple of years earlier. Hewey had at first resisted, mostly because he did not want to deal with the purchase of chickens or the building of chicken houses, but in the end he had actually done very little as far as the chickens were concerned. He did enjoy the eggs, along with the fried chicken they had most Sundays after the bible study held under the big mesquite tree that stood behind Aparicio's house.

Lanternlight showed through the lone glass window on the front wall of the bunkhouse, but none of the hands had yet emerged. Hewey was not concerned; they would soon enough if they wanted breakfast. He did it congenially, but he insisted horses be saddled before breakfast. That way the cowboys could ride out early enough to get something done in the cooler morning hours. It typically only took a couple of missed breakfasts followed by a long day to change the habits of those with a tendency toward sleeping late.

"Buenos dias," came Aparicio's voice from the darkness behind Hewey. "How is the leg today?"

Hewey never voluntarily talked about his injuries and disliked that the effects could still be seen. "A little stiff, but it'll limber up directly," he responded.

Aparicio struck a match and lit a lantern inside the saddle house. Within a couple minutes the other cowboys came up in ones and twos, just as twenty-one head of horses trotted out of the darkness and into the dim corral. Enrique Rodriguez followed behind the horses, riding a fidgeting bay colt that would have rather gone with its companions than follow Enrique's subtle commands.

As the youngest of the crew, it was Enrique's job to jingle up the day's mounts every morning. The chore demanded the teenager rise an hour earlier than everyone else, saddle his night horse, and then ride out and find the saddle horses in the half-section horse trap just beyond headquarters. The horses were easy enough to gather but always declined to come in of their own accord.

Most of the horses were gentle enough that the men walked up and easily caught them with rope halters. Three of the snortier broncs had to be roped. Many ranches roped every horse, regardless of its disposition. Hewey had given up on the tradition simply because it took too long.

It never occurred to him, although it did to several others, that it had not been too many years earlier that Hewey Calloway would have always chosen fun over efficiency. He would have roped every horse, efficiency be damned. The old Hewey was still there, but age and responsibility were quietly beginning to make their marks.

Hewey caught a short and wide dun gelding that had been broken the year before. He thought a lot of the dun and had named it Pincushion after he and Aparicio had spent an hour one morning pulling thorns out of the colt's side. It had evidently rolled on one of the harsh little cactuses. The dun was fortunate it had not stepped on the pincushion. The thorns were mean enough to cripple a horse.

Aparicio had put the first thirty rides on the dun before turning it over to Hewey. That had been a difficult adjustment for Hewey, but the old injury forced his decision. He decided the ability to walk was more important than riding broncs. Deep down he knew his leg might not hold up if he suffered another severe accident.

Pincushion had a hump in his back big enough to raise the snakeskin-covered cantle of Hewey's saddle by a couple inches, but Hewey was not concerned. The dun would probably let down by the time breakfast was over, and if not, Hewey knew he could still ride one if necessary. He wasn't *that* decrepit.

The men filed into the little building that served as the cook shack and mess hall. Blas Villegas was setting out breakfast—biscuits, refried beans and bacon. The women took care of the chickens and thus had first shot at the eggs. Every couple of days there were enough eggs for all the cowboys. This was evidently not one of those days.

Hewey had worked for many foremen and wagon bosses who said little of their plans for the day. The cowboys working for those men followed their silent lead and never asked questions. It was not in Hewey's nature to be such a foreman. He took his responsibility seriously, but it had not been so long ago that he was just one of the regular cowhands. He still enjoyed that camaraderie and felt no need to be a hardcase.

Most mornings Hewey lingered at the breakfast table over another cup of coffee, just long enough to outline the day's plan. It was his plan, and the men really had no say in it. But he could tell they appreciated his way of discussing things with them. They seemed to feel a part of the operation and not just a tool used in it.

Hewey sent his crew off in two directions. Three cowboys rode out to check windmills and tanks, but most were headed a few miles away to ride through a couple hundred head of heifers that were calving. Those heifers were dropping their first calves, and there had been a few difficulties, a few calves that needed pulled. Aparicio was in charge. Perhaps not everyone liked that, but they all knew it.

Although he preferred to spend his days working with his men, Hewey needed to ride some ten or twelve miles northeast to the Slash Y headquarters and talk to the foreman about the upcoming fall works. The two ranches combined forces and helped each other twice every year, during the spring and fall. The practice was called neighboring and allowed each ranch to get those labor-intensive works done without hiring outside help. Few ranch owners were big on writing unnecessary checks. Morgan Jenkins was not one of those few.

Once the cowhands headed off, Hewey headed east along the two-rut trail that led out of the ranch. In a few miles it would intersect the larger road that connected Alpine with the booming mining town of Terlingua, which was located to the south along the Rio Grande.

Pincushion had a smooth trot, but even so Hewey knew his leg would be sore by the time he made it home late in the day. However, he was grateful he could still ride twenty miles. There had been a time he worried he would never ride again.

The morning sun was warm on Hewey's face as he neared the Circle W's eastern fence and the road beyond. When he crossed a small hill just west of the road, he saw an automobile parked outside the fence and a man struggling to open the wire gate that led into the ranch. Hewey rode nearer and saw the man was a stranger. He was older than Hewey by a decade or so, soft in the middle and wearing a dark suit and a snap-brim driving cap.

Although Morgan Jenkins occasionally visited the ranch in his automobile, Pincushion had certainly never been this close to one of the machines. He snorted and sidestepped, threatening to do something untoward. Unconcerned with the horse's feelings, Hewey swatted the dun on the hip with the heavy tail of a rein. Pincushion decided Hewey was more of an immediate threat than the vehicle, and he moved forward cautiously.

The gate was made of five strands of barbwire with a cedar stay tied in the middle and another at each end. The gate fastened with two loops of barbwire, one at the top and another at the bottom. The gate had to be pulled tighter, by hand, to release the wire loops that held it closed. The man in the suit was having trouble with the task. He looked up as Hewey approached.

"Mornin'," Hewey said cautiously. He and Pincushion both eyed the stranger with some wariness.

"This is the Circle W Ranch, is it not?" asked the man abruptly. "I am looking for a man by the name of Hewey Calloway. Do you know where I might find him?"

Hewey thought that one over for a moment. The man did not strike him as a lawman. In any case, he had been on the straight and narrow, for the most part at least, since Spring had expressed her dislike of public drunkenness and the misfortunes that so often befell Hewey during those occasions.

"Yes, sir," he said finally. "This is the Circle W, and I'm Hewey Calloway."

"That is excellent news," said the man. "My name is Howard Stephens. I am an attorney in Alpine, for the time being at least. I have some information for you, and some paperwork. Would it be possible for us to go someplace where we might sit and talk? Somewhere out of this sun? It's getting dreadfully hot already."

Everything Hewey knew of lawyers taught him to be wary. "What do we need to talk about? Am I in some sort of trouble? I been behaving myself pretty well for a couple years now."

"No, Mister Calloway. I assure you this is all good news. I guarantee it, to be precise, but it is a bit lengthy to get into out here."

Hewey was still uncertain, but his curiosity got the best of him. "We can go up to headquarters. It's just a few miles thataway." He nodded his head west.

"Perfect," said Stephens. "Now, would you mind helping me with this gate? It seems to be broken."

Chapter Two

Hewey hurried back to headquarters, loping Pincushion much of the way. Even so, the lawyer Howard Stephens still beat him by several minutes. When Hewey rode up, Stephens was drinking a glass of tea on the porch of the big house. Spring and Olivia sat near him, although the conversation was limited. Little Elena stood in the yard staring at the black automobile.

Pincushion eyed the vehicle again, but he was more agreeable with the fresh ridden off him. Hewey loosened the cinch so the colt could breathe more easily, then wrapped a rein over a forked cedar post set in the hard ground outside the yard.

Olivia did not know what was happening, but she could tell it was something serious that did not involve her. She told Spring she would be next door and said goodbye to Stephens.

"Buena suerte, patron," she said as she passed near Hewey.

"You're the one goin' to need the luck, you keep calling me that," Hewey replied good naturedly.

He stepped up onto the wooden porch, where Spring eyed him curiously. Stephens had not told her or Olivia anything other than that he was an attorney and had business with her husband. Stephens had assured her that his news was positive, but she was still concerned.

"It's probably cooler out here in the breeze, but we can go inside if you want," Hewey said to the lawyer.

Stephens pulled at his collar. "Let's sit out here, if you don't mind. I thought it was hot in Alpine, but good Lord, this is something else."

Spring and Stephens each sat in wooden porch chairs. Hewey was too nervous to sit. He leaned against a big cedar porch post and eyed Stephens.

"Now, Mister Calloway, as I said earlier, I am an attorney in Alpine. I was hired by an attorney in Durango, Colorado, who thought it preferential to hire someone local rather than make the trip to handle things himself. He and I have had several telephone conversations, and yesterday a package arrived via the U.S. mail system."

Hewey wished the man would get to the point, but manners kept him silent.

"They tracked you to here through your brother Walter, who reportedly was very hesitant to give up your location at first. He thought you might be in some sort of trouble." Stephens looked at Spring, then back at Hewey. "Several people seemed to have automatically believed you were in trouble of some kind."

Hewey held up his hands defensively. "Hell, I don't know where they'd get that idea."

"Regardless," said Stephens. "I assume you

remember a family from Colorado by the name of Henderson?"

Hewey scratched his chin, thinking, and then grinned when it finally came to him. "He got shot by those outlaws me and Hanley were followin'. I hauled him down the mountain. They were nice folks."

"I have not met them, but considering why I am here today, I would have to say yes, they are apparently nice folks," said Stephens.

Spring was frowning at them, not understanding where this was headed. Stephens saw this. "Mrs. Calloway, are you familiar with the Hendersons?"

"Only through Hewey's stories," she replied. "Which are occasionally, well, embellished."

Hewey snorted, feigning insult. He could hardly deny it, though.

"I will tell you what I know, which I believe to be entirely accurate," Stephens said. "Approximately nine years ago our clients, Nate and Martha Henderson, were a young couple struggling to make it on a small stock farm in southern Colorado. While stealing the Hendersons' horses, three outlaws shot Mister Henderson and left him for dead. Mrs. Henderson was not injured but was left in a dire situation. It seems your husband and a Mister Hanley Baker were trailing these outlaws and came upon the scene. Your husband hauled Mister Henderson off the mountain in a wagon and then on to a local curandera. Mister Henderson subsequently survived the gunshot wound. The couple believes Mister Henderson would not have lived if it had not been for Mister Baker and Mister Calloway. Were you familiar with these events?"

Spring nodded. "Yes, that is very nearly exactly what Hewey told me. Several times." Hewey's favorite stories were those that cast himself in a favorable light, and he often had difficulty remembering the others.

"See," Hewey grinned. "That story don't need no embellishment."

"Yes, well," said Stephens uncomfortably. "Did Mister Calloway also tell you of the reward money he and Mister Baker received from the mining company?"

"Reward? No, he did not." Spring had always known that she loved Hewey for who he was and that she should not attempt to change him. He would resent it, and possibly her for trying. So, she had not attempted to change him, excepting one thing— Hewey's cavalier attitude toward money. If he could not spend it immediately, he often just gave it away. She appreciated his generosity to those in need, but she often felt *they* were the ones in need.

Hewey knew this. Although the reward money incident had happened years before he first met Spring, he had always felt it was a story best kept to himself. He had a feeling she just would not understand.

"Well, it is pertinent to my being here," said Stephens, picking up on the mood. "The mining company paid Mister Baker and Mister Calloway five hundred dollars in reward money for apprehending the men who had robbed the payroll. It seems that Mister Baker and Mister Calloway in turn donated the entireties of their rewards to the Henderson family."

"Hewey!" Spring blurted sharply. "You gave away five hundred dollars?"

Hewey raised his hands in front of himself defensively. "Nope. My half was just two-fifty. I didn't need it, and them folks was in rough shape right then. They were tryin' to make it on that little farm, and then he got shot. Me and Hanley thought it was the right thing to do."

After a short pause, he added, "The Christian thing." Spring gave him a dirty look.

"Yes, well, if I may continue," said Stephens. "I have information I believe neither of you know. The Hendersons saved that reward money and soon used it to purchase two-hundred-and-forty acres of land adjacent to their farm. I'm sure you are aware that there is a considerable amount of gold mining in southern Colorado. Well, Mister Henderson happened to find some color, which brought him to a sizable vein that led into the mountainside. It produced generously for several years, and I am told it is still producing smaller quantities today."

"I'm proud for them," said Hewey. "I liked those folks."

"It seems they liked you, also," said the lawyer. "The Hendersons used their gains to make other investments, mostly in mining and real estate. They now own a rather large hotel in Denver. They have done quite well financially. Very, very well, I am told. They believe much of their success is due to you and Mister Baker, because your generosity those years ago began their ascent. They now wish to repay the favor you did for them."

Hewey swatted away the notion. "Oh, hell. I didn't do that thinkin' I needed repaid. It wasn't a loan. It was a gift. They sent you all this way to give me back my two-hundred-fifty dollars?"

"Well, as a matter of fact they did not," said the lawyer. "It is more complicated than that. They feel it is more a matter of scale, you might say. You gave them this gift in 1904. How long would it have taken you to earn two-hundred-fifty dollars in 1904, Mister Calloway?"

Hewey thought about that. Arithmetic had never been his strong suit. "I don't know right off. I was gettin' about thirty a month probably. Cowboy wages. Why?"

"I was instructed to explain it to you this way, Mister Calloway," said Stephens. "The Hendersons wanted you to understand their thought process and how they came to this decision."

Spring had moved to the front of her chair but remained silent.

The lawyer went on. "They calculated that it would have taken you close to six months to earn that much money, so they understand the gravity of your generosity. You and Mister Baker each gave them an amount it would have taken you half the year to earn. They wish to pay it back on a similar scale."

Hewey began to pace along the front of the porch. This was quickly becoming complicated. "What are you sayin', mister?" he asked.

"The current price of gold, Mister Calloway, is $20.67 an ounce. I am told that the Henderson mine was producing, at its height, about one pound of gold per day. I know nothing of mines, but that does not even seem like a large amount to me. That is, until you do some calculations."

Spring looked as if she might begin to pace alongside Hewey. She wanted Stephens to get to the point. Surely he had one.

Stephens paused, either for effect or possibly to make himself certain this was all correct. He was still somewhat incredulous, and more than a little jealous. He had gone over it many times, though. "Since the Hendersons feel this is a matter of scale, they wish to give you and Mister Baker each approximately what the mine produced in six months, the time it would have taken you to earn what you gave them. That mine was producing, after operating expenses, a little over nine thousand dollars per month. So, they wish to pay you back with fifty thousand dollars. Each."

Spring gasped, and Hewey quit pacing. He was uncharacteristically silent for nearly a full minute. Spring studied her husband. Stephens perceptively kept quiet, giving Hewey time to think.

After a while Hewey began smiling, then burst out laughing, looking from Spring to Stephens. "Who put you up to this, mister? I bet it was that derned Snort Yarnell. That scoundrel always liked a good joke."

"I assure you, Mister Calloway, that this is no practical joke. Believe me, I am just as surprised as you are. Well, perhaps not quite as surprised, but surprised nonetheless."

Stephens could not say it just then, but it irked him that this cowhand was being given such an opportunity. This fool would probably drink it up or mismanage it into the ground in short order. The lawyer had never carried much respect for cowhands, or for common folk in general.

Hewey studied Stephens intently. He had never had much trust for lawyers, or for men who chose professions that required them to wear suits and strange hats and sit inside all day. "You're not trying to fool me somehow?" he asked.

Stephens sighed. "No, Mister Calloway. There is no joke or trick at play here. I realize this may come as a shock, due to the size of this gift, but it is real. It is just as I have explained it."

Hewey looked at Spring, searching for guidance but finding none. His expression hardened with resolve and perhaps even a touch of sadness. He turned toward Stephens. "No sir. I cannot in good conscience accept this. I gave that money to those folks as a gift. Not a loan. We're happy here and don't need handouts. Tell them thank you, but no."

Spring was not fully surprised, knowing her husband as she did, but she still did not like it. "Hewey," she said sternly. "Think about this for a minute at least."

"Hold on a moment!" Stephens held up a commanding hand, interrupting them. "There is more I must tell you. Mister Hanley Baker was much easier to locate, as he is much closer geographically to our clients than are you. My counterpart, the attorney in Colorado, traveled to Wyoming several weeks ago and spoke with Mister Baker. He at first declined their offer but reportedly changed his mind at the insistence of his wife."

A lifelong bachelor when Hewey first met him, Hanley Baker had met his future wife while he and Hewey were in Wyoming several years earlier. Baker had met Samantha Dearing while they were helping Bob Wilson. When they had Wilson's trouble sorted out, Hanley Baker had headed straight back for Cheyenne and the woman with whom he was smitten. Dearing was an extremely attractive woman whose wit matched her looks, and she was not shy about flaunting either of them.

Hewey had been invited to their wedding not quite a year later, but the letter did not find him until a couple months after the event had taken place. That had been the perfect excuse for his absence, he had felt then.

The Blessing

Hewey had not seen his old friend in eight years. Baker had written him a handful of letters, and Hewey had grudgingly responded when Spring forced the issue. Still, he felt like he knew Baker well and was surprised the old Ranger had accepted the money.

"Hanley took it?" he asked.

"Yes, Mister Calloway, he did. I hear his wife was quite," the lawyer paused a second, then finished, "persuasive."

A goofy grin crossed Hewey's face as he remembered Samantha Dearing. He knew what the lawyer meant by "persuasive". Spring had never met Samantha and frowned at her husband, wondering where his mind had gone. He had never described Samantha as anything other than "a real nice lady".

Stephens cleared his throat. "Personally, Mister Calloway, I can see no reason why your friend Hanley Baker should not have accepted this offer, or why you would not either, for that matter."

"Neither can I," Spring added.

"Mister Baker is evidently a perceptive man," said Stephens. "He advised my Colorado counterpart that you would almost certainly refuse the offer. I doubted that myself, but it now seems he was correct and that I was not. Mister Baker had a conversation with the Henderson family, and they came up with an alternate plan. A plan that has already been executed and one that will be much more difficult for you to simply turn down."

Hewey began to feel like he was being pressured into something he did not want, even if it was a generous gift. Spring sensed the shift in his mood and walked to him, placing a gentle hand on his shoulder. She did not want her husband kicking Stephens off the front porch before the man got to the point.

"What is this plan, Mister Stephens?" she asked quietly.

"They bought land, Mrs. Calloway. They felt your husband might be less likely to turn that down, and even if he wished to, the sale is already final. It belongs to the two of you now. You could sell it, or give it away I suppose, but for the moment it is yours. The sale was recorded. The deed was transferred. It is done."

Hewey again fell silent. He simply did not know what to say. In recent years he had begun to wonder what it might be like to own a little ranch, to have a permanent home for Spring. But those thoughts had immediately been pushed away. It sounded more like a burden than a blessing to him. It always had. He could not give up his freedom.

"Where is this land, Mister Stephens?" asked Spring.

"Upton County," said the lawyer. Hewey looked up at him, surprised yet again. "We found land for sale there, a portion of a large ranch that is being divided after the death of the owner."

Stephens shuffled through his papers until he found the copy he was looking for. "You're likely familiar with the place, Mister Calloway. We know you have family in Upton County, so that is where we began our search. We were fortunate to find something so suitable, and so quickly."

The lawyer pointed at the top sheet of his papers. "Yes, here it is. The ranch was evidently owned by a Mister C.C. Tarpley. The seller is listed as a Mister Frank Gervin. It seems Mister Gervin is keeping a portion of the ranch, including the headquarters, I am told. But he happily sold us this portion. I hope you and this Mister Gervin are friendly, Mister Calloway, because you will soon be neighbors."

"Oh hell," Hewey groaned pathetically.

Hewey stood quietly, digesting all that had just been told to him. Finally, he looked up at Stephens and surprised him, but not Spring, when the first thing he asked was, "When did old C.C. die?"

Stephens was momentarily confused. "I'm sorry, Mister Calloway. I am not familiar with this person." Then he remembered. "Ah, yes. C.C. Tarpley, the former owner. I do not know the date. I am sorry."

"C.C. must not have been gone long or I'd have heard, I reckon," Hewey said. The thought made him sad. C.C. Tarpley was cantankerous at times, but Hewey had always liked the man. "I'm not surprised it didn't take that son of a bitch Fat Gervin long to start selling C.C.'s ranch."

"Hewey!" Spring admonished. She preferred that he not use rough language in the house.

"What?" Hewey asked. "I'm on the porch, and Fat is a son of a bitch."

Spring rolled her eyes at him, then turned to Stephens. "What exactly did this couple, the Hendersons, buy for Hewey?"

The lawyer shuffled through his stack of papers, then stopped and read from one of them. "I do not know all the details of the negotiations, as I was not involved in that portion of this arrangement. I do know that this Mister Gervin was originally asking a good deal more per acre for the ranchland, but when he was presented with an offer for such a sizable amount of land, and with a letter from our client's bank guaranteeing their financial status, he quickly became more agreeable as far as price."

"Same old Fat," muttered Hewey.

"Yes, well, we discovered that it was only some twenty-five years ago that the railroad gave away a very sizable tract of land that is not far from your new ranch. The railroad simply deeded it over to the University of Texas. The railroad believed it to be worthless. That was used as a negotiation tactic with your friend, Mister Gervin."

Hewey frowned severely at Stephens. "He's no friend of mine."

The lawyer grew uncomfortable once more. "Certainly. The purchase in the end was for twenty-five sections of land, or close to it. As I believe I mentioned earlier, the larger ranch headquarters is not part of the purchase. There is, however, a smaller house with another couple of buildings and some sort of corrals. It is listed here as 'The Simmons Ranch Headquarters'. Mister Gervin initially valued these improvements outrageously high, but he eventually lowered the price."

Hewey smiled. "That's old Bill Simmons' place. I didn't even know C.C. had bought it, but I reckon I shouldn't be surprised. He owned everything up to it, and he always bought everything he could get his hands on. It's not much of a headquarters, but it's a decent place."

Hewey looked at Spring. "You ever been there? It's about ten or twelve miles southwest of Walter and Eve's house, straight south of C.C.'s ranch."

Spring shook her head. "I remember hearing of Mister Simmons, and I may have met him once, but I was never at his ranch."

"It's a nice spot. Got some trees and a windmill or two at the headquarters, with some good corrals and one barn. There's a rocky hill not far away. Simmons had two Mexican cowpunchers who could lay rock, and they hauled rocks from that hill and used it to build the house. Seems like there was a little shack for a cowboy or two. It's been a while since I was there."

There was a touch of excitement in Hewey's voice that did not go unnoticed by Spring. Then he began frowning as a thought crossed his mind. "All that land won't do us much good. We don't have any money to buy cattle to put on it."

Stephens cleared his throat. "Hold on, Mister Calloway. I was not finished. The contract states that the ranch comes with the cattle currently living on it. That was part of the negotiations, and I was told it was quite an ordeal to nail down Mister Gervin on the specifics regarding that point."

Once again, the lawyer looked over his papers until he found the correct paragraph. "The contract states that in addition to the fixed assets—the houses, corrals, windmills and such—the sale will include all livestock currently running on the ranch. The cattle were described as Hereford and Hereford-Longhorn cross. Mister Gervin estimated the stocking rate at one cow per thirty acres, which would bring the total number to approximately 500 head."

"That old C.C. Tarpley always run more than one cow per thirty acres," Hewey said, thinking back. "He thought it was a sin to waste a blade of grass."

"I can only say what is in the contract," said Stephens.

"Don't look a gift horse in the mouth, Hewey," added Spring.

"I'm not complainin'," Hewey said, again holding up his hands defensively. "I'm just tellin' you Fat needs to be watched pretty close."

"That is beyond my scope," said the lawyer. "All

I know is what is listed in this contract, and what I have been told. I was told nothing about Mister Gervin. I do not believe it has any bearing here."

"So," said Spring. "Hewey gets the land and the cattle, all free and clear?"

"Yes. As I said, the land and all the cattle on it. The land was basically valued at two dollars and fifty cents per acre, the cows at about fifteen each. The numbers add up, I assure you."

"I'm not questioning that," said Spring. "I'm just surprised by it all. Shocked even."

"You're not the only one, Mrs. Calloway." Stephens shuffled through his papers, extracted one and handed it to Hewey. "Here is a copy of the survey, so you will know the boundaries of your land. The sale is final, so you are the current owner. It is in your name, but I was informed that you will need to go by the courthouse in San Angelo to sign some paperwork. They likely want to get you nailed down so they may collect property taxes."

"Property taxes?" asked Hewey.

"Welcome to the real world, Mister Calloway," said Stephens.

Hewey studied the copy of the survey Stephens had handed him. It took him a couple of minutes to get his bearings and figure out exactly where the surveyed land lay in relation to the rest of C.C. Tarpley's ranch.

Hewey had worked for Tarpley several times over the years and was familiar with the ranch in general. He had never worked for Bill Simmons, so he was not too familiar with the details of that ranch.

He had begun grinning, although he did not realize it. Spring watched him silently, happily.

"C.C.'s best country was on the north end, up closer to Walter's place," Hewey said. "But the south end was always some of my favorite country. It gets rougher down there. There are more little hills and draws. It's pretty down there, in its own way. Gets a little sandy on the west side, but that don't hurt nothin' unless the wind's blowing."

Stephens began to look impatient, and when Hewey paused, the lawyer went over a few more details. It was obvious he was anxious to be on his way. He had pegged Spring as the more responsible of the two, so he handed her a stack of papers. "There is a copy of the deed, the sales contract and another copy of the survey. I believe it is everything you will need to move forward from here."

Stephens looked uncomfortable again, and he told them he had been asked to relay a short message to Hewey, from Martha Henderson herself. He told them he did not fully understand the message, but perhaps Hewey would.

"All it says here is that she once talked to you of priorities and perspectives, and that even in their good fortune they never forgot theirs," Stephens said. "She asks that you do the same, to remember as you did before."

Spring looked quizzically at Hewey, who was lost in thought and did not notice. He just stared into space, remembering a conversation from nearly a decade earlier. Martha Henderson had just told him she had torn up her only set of bed sheets for the bandages she used on her wounded husband. That one set of bed sheets had meant so much to her, up until the moment her husband had been shot.

Stephens gathered his remaining paperwork and placed it in his case, then stood. A trickle of sweat ran down one side of his face. "It has been a pleasure," he said unconvincingly. "My address in Alpine is listed on the paperwork. Please write or stop by if you have further questions."

Spring and Hewey remained on the porch, and they watched as Stephens got his automobile started. It took him several laborious turns of the crank on the front of the small car before the engine sputtered to life, disturbing several hens that had wandered near. Stephens saluted as he drove away, heading east down the dirt road toward town.

"What in the hell just happened?" asked Spring.

"No bad language in the house," reminded Hewey.

"We're on the damn porch," she corrected.

Hewey spent much of the afternoon pacing,

wandering around the barn and corrals aimlessly, trying to make sense of it all. Finally, late in the afternoon he saddled a bay colt that had been left in the corral. He rode away with no particular destination in mind. His thoughts had always come to him best while on a horse.

Early that evening he returned to headquarters and casually tied the bay colt outside the barn. He loosened the cinch but left the colt saddled. He needed to talk to Spring while the decisions were fresh on his mind.

He found his wife sitting at the empty kitchen table, staring blankly at the time-worn planks that made up the tabletop. She was silent, but a couple of tears slowly made their way down her cheeks.

"What's wrong?" Hewey asked gently as he sat in the chair next to her.

She looked over at him, her eyes glistening as new tears formed. "I don't know. All this." She waved her hand vaguely at nothing in particular. "We just found out that all of a sudden you're the owner of a ranch. A big ranch. This will change our lives, Hewey. It's wonderful news."

Spring paused to wipe away the tears that fell down her cheeks. "I can tell you're excited, even if you don't say it yourself. But you know what? As wonderful as this is, I don't even really care. It's not what I want. I'd stay here with you forever. I'd live down here with the heat and the scorpions and the snakes, if we could just have a family. That's all I want.

You know that."

Spring burst out crying, and Hewey grabbed both her hands in his own. A single tear fell from each of his eyes, which no longer surprised him. He had gone decades without shedding a tear, but his own longing, coupled with Spring's pain, had changed something in him. He still was not quite comfortable with it, but when it was only the two of them, he was no longer ashamed of his own emotions.

"I know it, Spring," he said quietly, wishing he could somehow give her the comfort she deserved. "I'd trade it all if I could. I just don't know who to trade with."

Chapter Three

Spring rose early with Hewey the next morning, knowing he would be gone for a couple days. She cooked them breakfast, which was a welcome treat for Hewey. She was not as liberal as Blas Villegas when it came to either peppers or grease.

She hugged him firmly before he left, then gave him a light kiss. "If you have time, go by the bookstore and bring me something."

Hewey smiled in the darkness. Spring had few material desires, but she liked her books. Hewey had even begun reading occasionally in the evenings. As a youngster he had enjoyed reading adventure stories about pirates and wild cowboys. It was a habit he had quit for over twenty years, but Spring had relit the fire.

He left at a trot, headed down the road that led out of the ranch. He had saddled Pincushion for the trip. He liked the dun colt, and this ride would be more miles than he cared to put on Biscuit. He still rode his old friend occasionally for easier jobs, but the brown had served his time. The young horses like Pincushion still *needed* the miles.

Aparicio had been left in charge again, so Hewey felt secure in being gone for a couple days. He was headed to Alpine, where he hoped to find Morgan

Jenkins and discuss the recent events and their plans moving forward.

The shadows were still long when he rode upon a large diamondback rattlesnake soaking up the early morning sunlight in the middle of the dusty road. The snake would soon be forced to seek refuge in the shade, but the morning was still reasonably cool. Hewey had always enjoyed wild animals and felt a sort of kinship with them.

That affection stopped just short of rattlesnakes. He harbored the same hatred for rattlesnakes that affected virtually all ranchers and stockmen who shared the country with them. Over the years Hewey had seen too many animals suffer through a slow recovery and occasionally a painful death following a snake bite. He always killed rattlesnakes wherever he found them, with neither compassion nor remorse.

Hewey slowed Pincushion to a walk when he spotted the big snake, which, at his approach, had coiled its body and raised its head. It did not rattle, but its tongue flicked in and out as it appraised them.

With his right spur Hewey nudged the dun toward the side of the road and continued on past. "Got no time for you right now," he said over his shoulder as he pushed Pincushion into an easy trot once again. "You better be gone by the time I come back, though."

The snake watched as the man and horse moved away and out of sight, then, paying no heed to Hewey's threat, it stretched out in the sun once again.

It was twenty-five or so miles to Alpine from the Circle W headquarters, and Hewey trotted into town by early afternoon. He could have pushed and made it faster, but he knew he would be staying the night anyway. There was no need to push the dun horse or his aching leg. He had plenty of time.

Alpine was a pretty town, Hewey thought to himself, which in turn struck him as strange. He had never much cared for towns, not after the first day or two at least. Towns had just never held his interest for long, particularly the older he became.

In his youth, which he had stretched to only a few years earlier, mentally at least, he had thoroughly enjoyed a good saloon and quite a few bad ones. He enjoyed them too much, it often turned out. Anymore, Hewey was just as likely to pass by a saloon as he was to stop, and when he did go inside it was only for a drink or two. Usually.

His breakfast back on the ranch had been eight or nine long hours earlier, so Hewey's first stop was a small cafe called Casa Azul. It was in an aging stone building just south of the railroad tracks, and Hewey had enjoyed it each of the handful of times he had eaten there over the last three years. The owners were originally from Mexico, friendly, and very talented in the kitchen. Hewey ordered the chile verde, which came with refried beans, rice and several warm corn tortillas. The pork cooked in green chiles was delicious, but it was so spicy Hewey drank three glasses of iced tea trying to cool the fire on his tongue. It did not help.

Alpine only held a few hundred people, so the ride from the cafe to Morgan Jenkins' place was short. Jenkins lived on the north edge of town in a nicer neighborhood. The house was large and made of native rock. Large trees shaded much of the house and most of the yard. There was a nice wooden barn with some pole corrals that had once held Jenkins' saddle and buggy horses. The corrals stood empty and appeared to have been so for quite some time. Hewey felt a touch of sadness as he studied the empty pens.

Jenkins' black automobile was nowhere to be seen, so Hewey assumed the man was not there. Ordinarily Hewey would have called out to the house from a distance, as tradition and manners demanded in most of the places he frequented. He did not figure that applied here, in town. The neighbors were just as likely to think he was calling to them as to Jenkins. So, Hewey shyly knocked on the door, hoping to find out where Jenkins had gone or when he might return.

Hewey heard voices from inside and a couple minutes later the door finally opened. Morgan Jenkins looked sleepy, as if the knocking might have woken him from a nap. He also looked surprised to see Hewey standing on his porch, and Hewey got the feeling the man might have been embarrassed to have been caught in the house during the middle of the day. Jenkins was old and prosperous, but he had spent most of his life as a working man. Those habits and attitudes were slow to fade.

Jenkins frowned at Hewcy, then demanded, "Hewey, what the hell are you doin' here? Somethin' wrong?"

Hewey had only been to Jenkins' home once. Nothing had been wrong then either, but his presence there was certainly not a common occurrence.

"No sir, nothin's wrong," Hewey answered. "Just need to talk to you about somethin'."

That caused Jenkins to frown even more. He was not big on mysteries. "Give me a minute. I need to get my hat."

Jenkins shut the door in Hewey's face without another word. Hewey moved a few feet away and sat on a low rock wall, waiting. He stretched his left leg in front of him, then drew it toward him, back and forth, trying to loosen up the knee. He quit when Jenkins emerged. The old man looked a touch brighter, with a hat on his head and a cup of coffee in his hand. He did not offer Hewey a cup. He might have, had it crossed his mind.

"Let's go 'round over here. Got some chairs," said Jenkins as he walked around the side of the house. Hewey followed to a courtyard of sorts, cool under the big shade trees. There were a couple of ancient wooden rocking chairs. Jenkins sat in one, and Hewey took the other.

"Well, what the hell you need to tell me? This ain't Sunday. You ought to be workin'," said Jenkins.

Hewey was not bothered by the old man's bluster. He had heard it many times. Jenkins was not all bad. He had a good heart, if a stingy one. He just preferred to hide his decency behind grouchiness.

It took Hewey nearly ten minutes to lay out the story for Jenkins, who went from impatience to interest to possibly even a touch of jealousy. No one had ever *given* him a ranch, after all. The rancher never said a word during the story, and when Hewey was done Jenkins sat quiet, frowning as he mulled it over.

"Damn, Hewey," the old man said finally. "I never heard of such a thing. They're just givin' you a ranch? That don't make no kind of sense to me."

"No," Hewey acknowledged. "Don't make much sense to me neither."

Both were silent, trying to figure it out. Finally, Jenkins asked Hewey the name of the lawyer, thinking he probably knew the man.

"Stephens. Can't think of his first name. I will in a minute," said Hewey.

"Don't know him, but I know of him. I never heard anything bad about him, other than he's a lawyer," said Jenkins, with no apparent humor. "I reckon this Gervin feller selling the ranch is the same son of a bitch who cheated me on those broncs a few years back?"

"That's him," Hewey agreed sadly. "I didn't even

know old C.C. was dead. It couldn't have been very long ago. Damned sure didn't take Fat long to start sellin' off the ranch."

There had been a time a few years earlier when C.C. Tarpley thought he was dying. Hewey talked him into seeing a doctor, and it turned out to be nothing but an ulcer. The last Hewey knew, Tarpley was still blowing and going. But that had been three, maybe four years earlier, Hewey realized.

"That's what son-in-laws are good for. Got two of them myself. Only one of them is worth a nickel. Hell, he probably ain't neither." Jenkins studied Hewey intently. "Speakin' of that, I felt sure you'd have a couple kids by now. I know there ain't much else to do down there once it gets dark."

A pained expression washed over Hewey's face, and he avoided the question. "You know I can't stay on with you now, even though I appreciate all you done for me after I got hurt."

"Well, I always tried to help out those in need when I was able. The Bible says a generous person will prosper and those who refresh others will themselves be refreshed. I believe much of my own prosperity is due to my own generous nature."

Hewey was doubtful. He figured Jenkins' prosperity had more to do with frugality than generosity, but he chose not to argue the matter.

"Things are goin' pretty smooth at the ranch," Hewey said. "It's as good a time as any for me to be leavin'."

Jenkins looked up at Hewey suddenly, as if he had a thought. "Hewey, how much money do you have right now? Not on you, but in a bank or a stash somewhere."

Hewey was surprised at the question. Most folks did not ask about the financial affairs of others, not without good reason. "Don't know exactly. Three, maybe four hundred," he said. "Spring stays after me about spendin' money, so I'm in pretty good shape, I reckon."

Jenkins rubbed his face with his hands and appeared unimpressed. "There have been many times when I had a lot less than that, I admit. But there's somethin' you don't seem to be thinkin' about. How many hands you think you'll need there on your new place?"

Hewey thought about that for the first time. "I don't know right off. Probably ought to have three or four, plus me, at least at first. I do know there will be more to do at first, just to get things right. We'll have to brand everything, even the cows and bulls."

"You'll need more hands than that if you start branding cows. That's hard work. I been there," advised Jenkins. "But what I'm gettin' at here is that you'll have to pay those men thirty a month, each, and you'll have to feed them. There will be other expenses you've never thought of, I can promise you that."

Hewey frowned at the thought of it all. These were

some of the reasons he never sought to own land of his own. He had always wanted to be a cow*boy*, but he had never sought to be a cow*man*. The difference was in the responsibility. He had seen the weight of it crush the spirit of good men.

He had no response, other than his burdened expression, so Jenkins went on. "I'm not tryin' to scare you here, Hewey. I'm just tellin' you that you're going to need an operatin' note from a bank. I get the feelin' you haven't thought of that."

"No, sir," admitted Hewey. "I hadn't."

"Well, I don't reckon borrowing money from that shyster Fat Gervin is a good plan, not for you anyhow. Soon as you can, go to a bank in San Angelo or somewheres else close and get yourself a line of credit. A couple thousand or so. Don't get so much that it's too hard to pay back. Knowin' you, it might be best if you put Spring in charge of it."

Hewey thought about that. He knew most men felt the need to be in charge of every aspect of the family, including, and even especially, the finances. That way of thinking seemed foolish to him. To start with, Spring was far better with figures than he was. Most importantly, if she handled the money, then it would be one thing he did not have to worry about.

"I might just do that," he said to Jenkins.

Jenkins suddenly had another thought, and he sat up and pointed an accusing finger at Hewey's chest. "I know most of them boys out there like you, Hewey.

Don't you be takin' any of them with you when you leave. I need 'em."

"I know it. Done thought of it," Hewey said. "I have to take Tommy, if he'll go. His mother's liable to shoot me if I show up without him."

Tommy Calloway, Hewey's youngest nephew, had been working for him the last couple years. Tommy had turned into an excellent hand, but Hewey worried about him constantly. The boy was too reckless for his own good. He must have got that from Walter, Hewey figured.

"You can take Tommy. I can't argue that one," said Jenkins. "You sure as hell can't take Aparicio. Can't have Blas either. If old Blas leaves, the rest of them will quit or else whine 'til I wished they had."

"I ain't plannin' to take them. Those two wouldn't go anyway. Blas is too old, and Olivia ain't going to let Aparicio move them that far from her family."

"All right, then. I don't know much about the rest of them boys, but I still need 'em all the same." Jenkins paused, thinking. "Reckon who I could get to run the outfit with you leavin'?"

Hewey had known this discussion was coming, and he had spent plenty of time thinking about it. "If it was me, I believe I'd put Aparicio in charge. He's been my wagon boss for three years, and he's as good a hand as I ever seen. He knows the country down there, too."

The old man stared at Hewey. "I know he's been the wagon boss, and I know some of them boys don't

like it. I ain't so old I don't know what's goin' on."
Jenkins paused, then said, "My momma's brother was
killed in the Battle of San Jacinto, just a few years
before I was born. What would she think, her eldest
son puts a Mexican in charge of the Circle W?"

Hewey knew he was on treacherous ground. He
didn't know exactly what Jenkins' mother might have
thought, but he figured he had a decent idea. "I
couldn't say about that," he said quietly. "I know
Aparicio wasn't at San Jacinto, though, and there ain't
a finer man or better cowboy around. Damned sure
ain't nobody better at the Circle W."

Jenkins stared at Hewey with an angry expression
on his lined face. "I know Aparicio wasn't at San
Jacinto, dammit. You know what I mean."

Hewey did know what Old Man Jenkins meant.
He wished it was not so, but it was. Not everyone felt
the same as he did. Knowing Jenkins' priorities, he
tried another tactic. "You put someone else in charge
down there and you'll feel it in your billfold. Things
won't run like they have been. I guarantee you that.
Some of the things we changed, things that made you
more money, those ideas come from Aparicio, not from
me."

That got Jenkins' attention. Nothing had ever
swayed him as quickly as a dollar. He thought about it,
frowning. Then he looked up at Hewey. "You reckon
Aparicio can keep a crew? Will the white men stay and
work for him? For a Mexican?"

Hewey sighed. The truth made him sad. "Not all of them, but maybe most of them. Some of them won't like the idea of working for a Mexican, but all except one or two respect him enough to stay, I reckon."

They both thought about that. Hewey asked, "You want my opinion?" Jenkins did not respond, so Hewey continued. "Them that won't work for Aparicio Rodriguez, you don't want them anyhow. Let 'em go. Aparicio will replace 'em with somebody better."

Jenkins studied on that for a long minute, his tired eyes staring into the distance. He had never thought of himself as a man bothered by the color of another man's skin. Over the years he'd had plenty of Mexicans and even a few black cowboys work for him. But, having one of them manage a ranch was another matter. People all over the country would be talking about him.

"You really think Aparicio would make me the most money?" the old man finally asked.

"I guarantee it."

"You get back down there, you tell them then," said Jenkins.

Morgan Jenkins had offered to let Hewey put up Pincushion overnight in his horse barn and corrals. Hewey was welcome to sleep in the barn too, Jenkins added. Hewey had not expected an invitation to the house, which was fortunate since Jenkins did not seem to have even considered it.

Payday for the month was not for another ten days, and Hewey had to bring up the fact that he was owed wages for about twenty days. The thought seemed to bring actual physical pain to Jenkins. His mood improved when Hewey told him he would like to buy Pincushion and also the buggy Jenkins had bought for him and Spring to use on the ranch. The buggy had been offered much like a gift, but Hewey knew it was a gift that was meant to be left at the ranch if he ever left.

"I'll swap you that dun even for what I owe you. For the buggy," Jenkins thought a moment, "I'll need forty dollars."

Jenkins was high on both counts, and both men knew it. Hewey grinned at the old man in an attempt to keep the mood light. He knew from experience that when Jenkins got mad, he also got stubborn.

"That buggy is about worn out from all the use it's seen on the ranch," Hewey said. "I'll give twenty dollars boot."

Jenkins was not fooled. "You can't outtrade me, Hewey Calloway. I bought that buggy when you was hurt, and I know damn well you hardly used it. It's practically new."

The two men stared at each other in silence for half a minute before Jenkins said he would trade for thirty dollars. Hewey agreed. They had both known all along that was about where they would end up.

The Blessing

The remainder of the day held little enjoyment for Hewey. He killed time as best he could, but he was anxious to head back to the ranch and get moving. He even considered riding back that evening. But it was a long way, and the ache in his leg told him he would pay for it for days to come if he pushed too hard.

The next morning Hewey was waiting outside one of the local cafes when it opened. It was a small place with good food at affordable prices that often drew cowhands when they were in town. The greasy breakfasts worked well to soak up the remaining alcohol from the previous night, so it had become a regular stop for most of them.

"You heard anything out of Snort Yarnell?" Hewey asked the gray-haired man he knew to be the owner. He could not remember the man's name.

Hewey was the only customer in the cafe at that early hour. The owner continued to cook his breakfast, trying to remember when he had last seen Snort.

"I can't rightly say," the man said finally. "It don't seem like he's been around lately, not in here at least."

Snort had worked for Hewey at the Circle W on two different occasions, neither lasting more than three months. It was a difficult situation for both of them. Hewey did not like telling Snort what to do, and Snort did not like Hewey telling him. No matter how diplomatically Hewey asked, it never went well. They had both finally decided it would be better for everyone concerned if Snort worked elsewhere.

Snort had left on good terms, but Hewey had lost track of him nearly a year earlier. His old friend might be a thousand miles away, or he might stroll through the door any second, gold tooth gleaming. Neither would much surprise Hewey.

"Say, if I left a note for Snort, would you keep it and give it to him next time he comes in here?" Hewey asked the cook. "I don't know no other way to get ahold of him."

"Sure thing," said the cafe owner, setting down a plate in front of Hewey. Fried eggs, bacon, fried potatoes, and three biscuits instead of two. The man had a good memory.

Chapter Four

Hewey and Pincushion trotted into the Circle W headquarters in the early afternoon. After a brief conversation with Spring, they decided to leave in two days. That would give them sufficient time to pack their few belongings. All the furniture belonged to the ranch, so they could easily pack their things in their new buggy.

They owned a pair of matched gray geldings that pulled the buggy. The horses had been a wedding gift from Alvin Lawdermilk three years earlier.

Olivia Rodriguez knew something was awry from their behavior, but she did not ask. They put off telling her until the late afternoon when Aparicio had returned. It was a conversation they preferred to have only once.

Hewey first spoke with Enrique Rodriguez and asked him if he minded riding down to the South Camp early the next morning to ask Tommy to come to headquarters.

Tommy had been at the camp with Jose Luna for several months. Hewey would have preferred that Tommy stay at headquarters where he could better watch out for him. But, when they needed another camp man, Tommy had volunteered and no one else did. Hewey did not like it, but he felt he couldn't treat his nephew differently than the other men. Despite Hewey's misgivings, Tommy had gone.

Enrique grinned when Hewey asked him to go to South Camp. It was something different to do, plus he and Tommy were friends. "Si, Mister Hooey," he said in heavily accented English. "I go now."

It was eight miles to the camp. "Tomorrow morning is fine," Hewey said.

Enrique shrugged. "No te preocupes. I go now," he said.

Hewey gave up. The boy was energetic and looking for something different to do. "Tell Tommy to bring all his stuff."

Enrique nodded. "Okay, Mister Hooey."

Aparicio, Olivia, Spring and Hewey gathered on the porch of the big house. Elena sat in Spring's lap. Hewey knew he should be the one talking, but he had trouble beginning. Everyone watched him expectantly.

"What's going on, patron?" Olivia finally prodded.

Hewey was too distracted to notice her tease. He sighed, then told them a brief version of what had transpired, stopping just short of telling them about Aparicio's new position.

Aparicio and Olivia were initially surprised, but it soon turned to happiness for their friends. Aparicio smiled broadly and slapped Hewey on the back.

Aparicio had always been perceptive, and he studied Hewey then. "This is good, my friend. This thing, it happened because you did something nice for those people a long time ago. You are good to other people all the time. I think maybe you need to remember this."

Hewey smiled weakly, trying to see it that way. He told Aparicio that Morgan Jenkins wanted him to run the Circle W and had named him as foreman. Aparicio appeared shocked, and Olivia began to cry quietly. She had always believed in her husband, but the fact was that many did not, solely because of the color of his skin. Concerned, Elena got up from Spring's lap and hugged her mother.

Uncomfortable with the situation, Hewey told Aparicio they had best go tell all the cowboys. Aparicio knew it must be done, but he would have preferred to sit and enjoy the moment a few minutes more.

Most of the cowboys were on the bunkhouse porch, but a couple were inside. Hewey asked them to gather outside, explaining that he had something to tell them. Blas Villegas heard the commotion and stepped outside the cookhouse to listen. Aparicio stood near Hewey, content to follow his friend's lead.

When everyone had loosely assembled, Hewey began by telling them he would be leaving the ranch in a couple days and that the next day would be his last as foreman.

"Where you goin', Hewey?" asked a good-natured cowboy named Francis O'Reilly.

Hewey did not want to go into detail. "We're headin' back to Upton County. Got family back there."

"What the hell you plannin' to do up there?" O'Reilly asked.

"Oh, we're goin' to take care of a ranch there, part of the old Two Cs," Hewey said. None of the men were familiar with the Two Cs, so that halted the questions, for the moment at least.

If trouble came, Hewey was certain it would come from one of two men, or possibly from both men. Slim Caldwell and Burt Barcheers had formed a friendship based mostly on general pessimism and a mutual dislike for those of other skin colors.

Hewey had often wondered why they stayed on at the Circle W, but they had for over a year. He would have preferred the two men move on, but they had not. They were both good hands, and despite some quiet grumbling, they had caused no real problems. Hewey did not like their viewpoint on race, but the fact was that it was 1913 in West Texas. He understood the facts, even if he did not always agree with them.

Caldwell had been looking from Hewey to Aparicio, frowning as he pieced it together. Caldwell was about forty, shorter than Hewey but broader. He was missing two top teeth for reasons unknown to Hewey. "Who's goin' to run the place when you leave?" Caldwell asked.

The Blessing

"I talked to Mister Jenkins about that yesterday. He wants Aparicio to take over as foreman. I recommended Aparicio, but it was Mister Jenkins that made the decision."

"I don't like it none," growled Caldwell as he glanced at Barcheers for support. "It's been bad enough with you playin' favorites. I reckon it'll be worse now."

"Well, ain't nobody forcing you to stay," Hewey said. "You can move on if you don't like it."

"I might just do that," Caldwell said, his temper quickly rising. "I ain't workin' for no goddamned greasy wetback."

Hewey rarely got mad. He never had, not really. It just was not his personality. But he did then, and it happened instantly, before anyone saw it coming. Caldwell had been standing a few feet in front of Hewey, but the man had taken a couple of aggressive steps forward as his own anger flowed, stopping just in front of Hewey.

When Caldwell called Aparicio a greasy wetback, something flashed in Hewey's eyes. He felt as if a fire was burning in his chest. It overwhelmed him. He had heard the grumbling about Aparicio, a man who was nothing but kind to everyone, and he had let it go. Now, it all came boiling up at once.

No one saw it coming, least of all Caldwell. He thought his taunts and complaints would be met with words, not violence. Hewey took half a step toward the bigger Caldwell, cocked his right fist and hit the man in the nose with everything he had.

Fighting had never been Hewey's best event, far from it, in fact. But that punch was thrown from the shoulder, and it was fueled by anger that had been building for a year. Blood spurted from Caldwell's nose. The man grabbed at his face as his knees went weak. He slumped to the ground, conscious but unable to catch himself.

Hewey stepped forward, intending to kick the downed Caldwell. Before he could deliver the blow, something struck him on the back of the head. It felt hard, much like a hammer, but as he fell to the ground, he wondered to himself why anyone even had a hammer. He landed next to Caldwell, who was still lying face down on the ground but was trying to rise using only one hand. The other hand was pressed to his gushing nose.

The anger over what Caldwell had said about Aparicio had not left Hewey, although he was dazed by the blow to his head. He crawled forward onto Caldwell's back, grabbed the man by his dirty brown hair and began pounding Caldwell's face into the hard, rocky ground.

Hewey was about to slam Caldwell's face on the ground for the third time when strong arms grabbed him from behind, dragging him up and backward, off Caldwell, who was no longer struggling.

"Bastante, amigo," came Aparicio's soothing

voice from just behind him. "I think maybe he's had enough."

Hewey struggled at first but finally relaxed. Aparicio released his arms. Hewey reached back and rubbed his head, where a sore knot had already formed. He turned around to see who had clobbered him and was surprised to see Blas Villegas holding a small, slim knife to the throat of Burt Barcheers. Blas carried the little knife in a leather scabbard on his belt and often spent his free time pulling the little blade across a leather strop. Everyone knew it was sharp.

Barcheers did not have a hammer, Hewey was surprised to see, but he was holding a fist-sized chunk of jagged brown rock he had apparently picked up off the ground.

Hewey studied Barcheers. "You know, Old Blas here has spent sixty, maybe seventy years," he trailed off, then asked, "How old are you, Blas?"

Blas looked at Hewey, his black eyes gleaming. He seemed to be enjoying the moment. "Estoy arto de esta mierda."

"Did you understand that, Barcheers?" Hewey asked. "I reckon probably not. Mostly it means that Blas has put up with sons of bitches like you and Caldwell for too long. Might be he's about to cut your throat."

Barcheers did not believe it, and his self-righteousness flared. "You wouldn't dare, Calloway, none of you would. The law would be down here and hang this Mex. This is Texas, by God."

Hewey smiled, but there was no humor in his eyes. "You think the law would even know?"

Still on the ground, Caldwell groaned as he tried to sit up. Barcheers looked at the men standing around, half of them white, half Mexican. He searched the white faces for allies. "Somebody here knows what's right and what ain't," Barcheers demanded.

A couple of the men looked at the ground, although several stared back defiantly at Barcheers. None spoke.

"Looks to me like you've run out of friends, Barcheers," Hewey said. "Now you gather up Caldwell and your gear and you leave, tonight. Right now. Turn him loose, Blas."

Barcheers jerked away when Blas lowered the knife, then he sullenly helped Caldwell to his feet and into the bunkhouse. The other men openly stared at Hewey. They had never seen this side of him.

Hewey looked at Aparicio and grinned broadly. His heartrate had slowed somewhat, and his temper was calming. He waved a hand at the cowboys standing in front of them. "You're a couple of men short, but it looks like we got the culls sorted off."

Aparicio shook his head sadly. "There will be more troubles, my friend. This job, it is a good thing, but yo prometo, this will not be the last of the problems."

"Ain't nothin' you can't handle." Hewey grinned,

then turned serious. "Say, you don't reckon either of them fellers has a gun in the bunkhouse, do you?"

If Caldwell or Barcheers had guns they chose not to use them. Francis O'Reilly rode out into the horse trap and brought up the remuda, so Caldwell and Barcheers could catch their personal horses. The two men saddled their mounts and rode away without exchanging a word with anyone. That suited them all.

Spring was initially unhappy when she learned of the fight, which did not surprise Hewey at all. Still, her anger quickly subsided when she learned the reason for the dispute. Olivia listened quietly, worry in her eyes. She knew this would not be the last struggle her husband would face in his new position, deserved or not. She said nothing, but with teary eyes she walked to Hewey and hugged him for what seemed to him like a long, long time.

The next morning Hewey stayed away from the saddle house and the cowboys, allowing Aparicio to take over without his presence. He watched the men leave in a trot, all but Aparicio, who walked to the big house to ask Hewey and Spring if they needed help with anything.

"There ain't much to pack," Hewey said. There really was not much, although Spring had already done most of the packing without him.

The sound of approaching horses brought the three

to the porch, where they found Tommy Calloway and Enrique Rodriguez walking their horses toward the saddle house. At the sight of their families, the young men veered toward the house.

Hewey was grinning at his nephew. "You two must've left pretty early to get here by now," he said.

"Shoot, Uncle Hewey, I left the same time I leave every day," Tommy said. "Two hours before daybreak."

Enrique smiled widely, looking from Tommy to Hewey. "Eso no es la verdad. Tommy is muy curioso about what's goin' on. He could not wait to get here."

"Get down, both of you, and I'll tell you."

The young men stepped down and held their bridle reins while Hewey gave an abbreviated version of the events. It was not his style to shorten a good story, but he was anxious to get moving and knew he would have plenty of time to tell Tommy the rest later, on the road.

"I'm sure Aparicio would keep you on here if you're set on it, but I know I'll need some good help myself." Hewey kept a straight face, staring at his nephew. "Until I can find some, I reckon I'll have to make do with you."

Tommy tried to act hurt, but he could not keep a straight face with Enrique laughing and poking him in the ribs. "You know, Hooey, you in bad shape I think," said Enrique. "Tommy is such a bad vaquero that he can barely drive gentle cows down a road with fences on both sides. I think maybe you better take me with you."

Hewey had felt certain this conversation with Enrique was coming, and he had dreaded it. He wanted to take the boy with him. He would need the help, and he knew it. But he had promised Morgan Jenkins he would not poach the man's cowboys.

"Shoot, Enrique, I'd like to have you. I really would. But I guaranteed Mister Jenkins that I would leave all his hands here, 'cept Tommy. Besides, your uncle is the patron now. He's going to need your help here."

Tommy and Enrique had not heard the news about Aparicio taking over as foreman. Tommy raised his eyebrows in silent surprise, and Enrique grinned, showing most of his surprisingly white teeth.

Enrique thought it over, and his grin slowly faded. "I think maybe Tio Aparicio will be okay without me. I think I go with you."

Hewey shook his head. "Dammit, Enrique, you're a hell of a good kid, but you don't listen for nothing. As much as I'd like to have you, you have to stay here." Hewey turned and walked toward the barn so he would not be forced to argue further.

Tommy looked at his friend and shrugged. Enrique winked at him.

Hewey saddled the roan colt for what he figured was the last time. The colt belonged to Morgan

Jenkins, and as much as he hated to, Hewey would leave him at the ranch when he left. He spotted Tommy and motioned him over.

"I'm gonna ride down and say adios to Skip," he said. "You want to come with me?"

Tommy nodded. "I thought of that, too. I'll go."

They each mounted their horses and rode southeast of headquarters across the valley for a little over half a mile. They stopped beside a wooden cross made of mesquite wood set in the hard desert ground. There were no words, fences or other markers, just the one wooden cross, standing alone in the open pasture.

Hewey and Tommy both stepped off their horses and stood, hats in hand, staring at the cross. It had been three years since Skip Harkness had died at the spot after he was gored by a Longhorn bull fleeing a losing fight with another bull. Skip, a foolish teenager, had set up the fight so he and the other cowboys could bet on the outcome.

The boy's body had been sent home to his parents, but two of the younger vaqueros had built the cross and erected it where Skip died. It was their way of honoring their friend. Mexicans, Hewey had come to learn, looked at death differently than most white people he had known. Loved ones were missed severely, but they were still often celebrated.

Skip had been Tommy's best friend at the time, and the boy had taken it hard. He had seen the accident happen, and he had even bet Skip which bull would win the fight.

Hewey had been in charge when Skip was killed. Although he had warned Skip and Tommy to be careful, he felt later that he should have been more forceful in stopping the foolishness altogether. Three years later the guilt still pressed upon him. He did not talk about it much, but it was there, festering within him, receding at times only to come roaring back without warning. Spring could see it but did not know how to help. Hewey did not believe anyone could, and he wasn't sure he wanted help anyhow. Deep down he believed he *deserved* to bear the guilt.

Every few days for the last three years Hewey trotted down to Skip's wooden marker. He preferred to go alone, so no one could see his tears or hear his words. He never said much, but he always told Skip he was sorry.

Hewey had planned to leave the next day, but by midmorning all they had left to do was say their goodbyes and leave. Biscuit had been loafing near headquarters all morning, and Hewey had not bothered to catch the brown horse until then.

After tying the rope halter, Hewey took a moment to study the horse's head, searching for gray hairs. He thought for a couple minutes, trying to figure out just how old Biscuit was then. He knew it was 1913, but he could not remember the year he had bought Biscuit.

At first he decided the horse must have just been about ten years old, but then he decided he must be missing a couple years somewhere. The horse was older than that. Biscuit had a lot of life and use left in him, but he had hit the point that Hewey did not think he could teach the horse anything else. Biscuit knew it all. He was finished and reliable.

Hewey had always enjoyed riding younger horses. He liked the excitement and also the pleasure of teaching a horse new things. It gave him a sense of accomplishment. On top of that, he had never wanted to become one of the older men forced by time to ride the older, easier horses. That was not who he wanted to be, not ever.

Several times over the years Hewey had turned down opportunities to sell Biscuit, a couple of them for more money than he had previously dreamed a horse would ever bring.

Hewey thought back to the previous fall, when Morgan Jenkins had visited the ranch with a Fort Worth cow buyer. Hewey had chosen to ride Biscuit that day because he knew he would be sorting whatever cattle the buyer selected, and he wanted to be mounted well for such a ticklish task. The sorting had been difficult, as Hewey had expected, due to the wild nature of the cattle and the argumentative natures of both the cow buyer and Morgan Jenkins.

Biscuit had done his job that day. True to form, it was done with a casualness that belied the true difficulty of the situation. Afterward, the cow buyer approached Hewey and asked what he wanted for the horse.

"I don't reckon I ought to sell him," Hewey had told the cow buyer.

The older man had offered Hewey fifty dollars then, which was a lot but not nearly enough. Hewey said no thanks. The man offered seventy-five then. Hewey said no thanks, although not so quickly as before.

"I need that brown for my grandson," the man had said commandingly. "I'll give you a hundred dollars, cash money, right now."

Morgan Jenkins told Hewey he better take it. Jenkins wondered why the cow buyer had not been so generous about the price of the cattle he had selected. Both the cow buyer and Morgan Jenkins had been mystified when Hewey politely turned down that offer and walked away before another could be made.

The sound of Elena's voice brought Hewey back to the moment at hand. He ran a hand along Biscuit's neck, then turned and led the horse to the yard in front of Aparicio's house. Spring and Olivia were sitting on the porch, the packing all done.

Elena was sitting on the edge of the porch in the shade, brushing the hair of one of her few dolls. She was humming quietly to herself as she played. Hewey walked up to her, leading Biscuit. He stopped a few feet away and watched her. Elena looked up at him, smiled happily, and then went back to brushing.

Hewey watched Elena for a full minute without speaking, trying not to get emotional, then he turned and looked at Biscuit standing quietly at the end of the lead rope. Hewey reached out and ran a hand along Biscuit's nose, then looked back at Elena.

Aparicio's voice startled him. Hewey had not seen him come from the corrals and cross the yard to him. "Hold on, my friend." Aparicio looked from Hewey to Biscuit and then to his daughter on the edge of the porch. "It is a nice thing, what you are planning to do. But I think maybeso you better keep Biscuit for your own family."

Dumbfounded at being so transparent and also by what Aparicio was implying, Hewey did not know what to say, so he just looked at his horse.

"I think maybe someday you gon' have a little boy, or God willing," Aparicio looked down at his daughter, "a little girl. When that time comes, my friend, you gon' need ol' Biscuit here. You will see."

Hewey still did not know what to say, and he did not feel like he could speak even if he had the words. He stood silent, staring at his horse. Finally, Hewey looked over and met Aparicio's eyes, his own glistening but not quite spilling over.

Aparicio patted him on the shoulder. "Esta bien, amigo. I understand."

Chapter Five

They left before noon, Hewey driving the buggy pulled by the two matched gray driving horses, their meager possessions stacked in the bed. Biscuit, Pincushion and the roan colt were all three tied to the back of the buggy, side by side.

Hewey had decided at the last minute he was taking the roan. He would need more horses than he owned, and the roan showed such promise. He and Aparicio had agreed on the price, and Hewey would mail the payment to Morgan Jenkins. The old rancher should be proud of his new foreman, Hewey figured, since Aparicio had gotten the better end of him in the horse trade.

Tommy rode alongside the buggy and sometimes behind, depending on the road, on a short-backed, compact sorrel he'd owned for a year or so.

After ten miles or so the wagon seat had become uncomfortable to Hewey, despite Spring having placed a folded blanket as a cushion. Hewey began to wish he was sitting in a saddle rather than the wagon seat. But that seemed unfair to Spring, so he stayed where he was.

They made camp that night just east of Alpine, after having stopped in town for a few supplies and a meal at the cafe. They would eat in camp enough over the next several days to justify eating in town when the opportunity presented itself.

Before they left town, Tommy quietly asked Hewey if it would be all right for him to stick around town for a while before heading back to camp.

"What are you plannin'?" Hewey asked.

Tommy kicked a small rock, acting slightly nervous, shy even. He looked at the ground. "I don't know. Thought I might go to a saloon, or somethin'."

Hewey grinned knowingly. He was not certain, but Tommy ought to be about twenty-one years old or so. "What do you mean, or somethin'?"

"I don't know, Uncle Hewey." Tommy had turned a bright shade of red.

"Just don't do anything foolish, and don't stay out too late. We're leaving at sunup, and tomorrow will be tough if you've still got a bunch of cheap whiskey sloshing around inside you. Believe me, I know."

Tommy grinned, relieved. "I don't plan on drinkin' too much."

"Yeah, I get the feelin' that's not what you're after," Hewey said. "I ain't tellin' that part to Spring, and your mother neither when we see her. Either one of them is bad enough, but Lord help us if they was to ever team up against us."

True to his word, Hewey had them rolling as the

sun appeared over the distant mountains the next morning. Tommy looked a touch peaked, as if perhaps his stomach was sour and his head fuzzy. Hewey figured it probably took Tommy several drinks to get up the nerve to pursue his main objective the night before.

After a few miles, Hewey grew bored and decided to poke Tommy. "What all'd you do last night?" he asked innocently.

Tommy shot him a worried look. "Oh, nothin' much. Just went to a couple saloons, looked around a little bit."

"What'd you see?" Hewey prodded.

"Just some saloons. Same as any, I reckon."

"Well, which ones did you go to?" I probably been there myself." He looked at Spring, who knew he was up to something, although she did not know what. "Before I was a married man, of course."

"Well, one was called the Bloated Goat," said Tommy. His forehead scrunched up as he thought. "I don't remember the name of the other one."

Hewey laughed aloud. "The Bloated Goat! You went there? What the hell for? Why, that place is known more for its professional ladies than its drinks. Hell, you should've asked me where to go. I could've told you the places with the better whiskey. Quieter sort of places, without those sorts of women in there tempting a good young boy like yourself. It's a good thing you're such a fine, rule-following *Christian* boy, else you might have done somethin' regretful last night."

Tommy stared at his saddlehorn, his face red and pained. Spring was not so naïve as to not catch on. Smiling, she sharply elbowed Hewey in the ribs. "Shut up, Hewey."

It took them four days to reach Upton County. The buggy slowed them down, which was working on Hewey's patience severely by about the middle of the trip. He longed to be horseback, where he could strike a lope and cover some country. The wheels would soon vibrate off the buggy if he loped the team, so he held them to a slow, mind-numbing trot.

They crossed a new railroad track running basically east and west in the far southern part of Upton County. There was more traffic than Hewey was used to, most of it along a road that followed the tracks. There was an occasional automobile, much to Hewey's irritation, but there was also more wagon and horseback traffic.

Finally, Hewey asked a young cowboy who was traveling the same direction as them but who had overtaken the buggy. After exchanging howdies and a couple other pleasantries, Hewey asked the young man why there was so much traffic on the road.

The man, a skinny cowboy with a scraggly, unkempt beard, slowed his bay horse to match the speed of the buggy. He looked at the empty road ahead, then turned his head and looked at the empty road behind. "Traffic?" he asked.

"Hell, I know it don't seem like much right now, but there's more than there used to be around here."

The cowboy scratched his thin beard. "How long since you folks been here?"

"About three years, I guess," Hewey said.

The cowboy nodded, realizing. "There's a new town up yonder a few more miles."

"A town?" Tommy asked from his horse on the other side of the buggy. There had not even been talk of a town the last time he was in the area.

"Yep," said the cowboy. "Been there a couple years or so. Ain't much to it. They call it Rankin."

"Damn," said Hewey. "What the hell they want with a town way out here?"

The young cowboy nudged his horse into a faster trot and eased away from them. Tommy voted to go see the new town, but Hewey dismissed the idea. "It ain't on the way. We're about to head north. I reckon you'll have plenty of chances to see it later."

Soon they turned off the road and headed vaguely north, following a dim wagon trail. Hewey had spent enough time in the area that he was familiar with the way to Bill Simmons' place. He thought about that for a spell. *His* place. The sound of it only confused him.

A couple miles north of the road they came to a barbwire fence with a gate across the wagon trail.

Tommy got off his horse to open it. Hewey stood in the wagon and looked across the pasture.

He motioned across the land, showing Spring. "This is it, right here. This fence marks the south end. The house is a few miles thataway." He pointed northeast vaguely. "There's a better way to the house from the east, but I wanted to go this way so we could cut across the place and look at it."

Spring looked across the pasture appraisingly. She had spent much of her life in West Texas and had developed a native's appreciation of the landscape, although she could still see it somewhat objectively. The land was broken by small, rough hills with sandy soil between them.

The grass was short nearly everywhere, a brown color with only a hint of green, a testament to the harsh, dry summer that so often plagued this part of the state. Low mesquite trees were scattered generously across the pasture, most of them more like bushes than actual trees. Yucca, catclaw and prickly pear were plentiful.

"It gets flatter as you go north," Hewey said. "The country gets better up there, but it's not as pretty."

Spring smiled at him. *Pretty?* she wondered. Still, she was struck, just as Hewey was, by a sense of excitement, even pride. She had grown up poor and had never been able to get away from it in adulthood. Material possessions had never meant much to her, but more than once she had wondered if that was because she had never owned many of them.

The Blessing

The going was slow across the ranch. The wagon trail had likely never been smooth, and the infrequent rains had been unkind to it in places. It was late afternoon when they drove up to the house and barns.

The house, true to Hewey's memory, was made of light-colored native rock. The roof had tin on it, which Hewey did not remember. There was a small bunkhouse made of the same rock. The barn was wood, large but with only one wall on the north side. A small wooden saddle house sat next to it.

There were several wooden corrals, most showing more wear than care in recent years. Hewey quickly decided they would hold some stock, so long as the stock did not try too hard to leave.

There was a sun-bleached outhouse, and near the barn a chicken house leaned to the east, the chickens long gone. There was nothing else but empty country, as far as they could see in any direction.

Hewey stepped down and casually tied the team of grays to a fence. He helped Spring from the wagon, and without words they both headed for the house. Both knew the other was curious.

Halfway to the porch a buzz sounded from underneath a catclaw bush in the yard. Spring and Hewey both stopped instantly, each all too familiar with the sound of a rattlesnake. They spotted the snake only a few feet away, coiled in the shade.

Tommy had heard the snake. "Hold on, let me find somethin'." He looked around and saw an ancient garden hoe leaning against the side of the porch. Most places around West Texas had a hoe or shovel on or near the porch to dispatch the rattlesnakes that were so often found too close for comfort.

Rattlesnakes were nothing new for Tommy, either. He casually approached the snake, maneuvered the hoe around a couple times for position, then chopped off the broad head.

He picked up the head with the hoe and dropped it into the center of the catclaw, where no one would step on it. Everyone had heard stories of how a rattlesnake's head could still bite and inject venom, even after the head had been separated from the body. Tommy had seen many of the heads still wiggling, as this one was, so he did not doubt that it could happen.

Tommy picked up the snake and held it up for Spring and Hewey to see. It reached from the ground to his chest. "Y'all want to eat it?" he asked.

Spring grimaced, but Hewey said, "I've ate a few. They're dang good, really, if you batter and fry them like a piece of chicken."

Spring was not convinced. "You two can do that, if you're of a mind, long as you do it outside. Not in my new kitchen."

Hewey grinned at her. "Oh, hell. You think that'd be the first rattlesnake ever been in that kitchen? I wouldn't be surprised if there ain't one in there right now."

The Blessing

They did not find a rattlesnake in the house, despite a thorough search insisted upon by Spring. The house appeared to have been inhabited recently, probably by a Two Cs cowboy or two. The ranch had likely used the place as a camp since it was ten miles or more to the Two Cs headquarters.

The house was fairly small, but it was stout and structurally sound. It had a wooden floor, worn smooth by time. The kitchen had some crudely built wooden cabinets, a wood-burning range and a rickety kitchen table with four chairs. There were two other rooms meant to be bedrooms. One held the frame of an old bed. The other was empty.

The entire house was covered in a fine layer of dust. Spring appraised it all in silence.

"I know it ain't much," Hewey reassured. "But it's yours, if you want it."

Spring looked at him, tears in her eyes. "I want it. It just needs a little bit of cleaning. Well, maybe a lot of cleaning."

"We'll go into Upton City tomorrow or the next day and get some supplies. I know we'll need some stuff." Hewey looked around. They needed so many things he did not know where to start, or how to pay for it all.

Spring looked at the smaller bedroom toward the back of the house. "Maybe someday we'll need to turn that into a nursery."

Hewey winced, but Spring was looking toward the

bedroom and did not see it. "I pray for it every day, same as you."

There were two windmills at headquarters, which was as unusual as it was nice. Surprisingly, both were still operating and pumping water. Hewey knew they had better check the oil in them soon, since there was no telling when it had last been done. That was a good job for Tommy, Hewey reasoned.

One of the wooden windmill towers was just outside the corrals at the barn, and it pumped directly into a dirt tank someone had likely dug with mules and a fresno. Hewey studied the setup, planning some improvements when time and money allowed.

The other windmill stood just behind the main house. The original ranchman, Bill Simmons, had evidently spent some time planning and building the water system.

The slow, uneven flow of water came out of the ground and spilled into a long rock trough that sloped gently toward the back of the house. There was a small metal spigot on the side of the trough, near the back door of the rock house. The house did not have running water, but at least the water did not have to be carried far.

To Spring's delight, another spigot drained into an ageless iron bathtub. The water would be unbearably cold unless boiling water was added, but it was still an uncommon comfort in ranch country. Hewey and Spring looked it over, testing the spigots and finding them stiff from unuse but still operating.

The tub sat in the open, and the scattered mesquites offered little concealment. Hewey said, "You start bathing out here, we'll have ever' boy and half the men in Upton County hidin' in the brush out yonder, watchin' the show."

"You among them, I'm sure," said Spring. "Well, at the top of your list of things to do is to build me a solid fence around this so I don't have to worry about that."

Hewey grunted. He had plenty to do already. Spring began cleaning as best she could with limited supplies, and Hewey stepped outside in time to see Tommy emerge from the saddle house with another dead rattlesnake draped from a worn shovel. He walked to the barn to look around.

"Sons of bitches are thick around here," Hewey said of the snakes.

Tommy was nonchalant. "Oh, I bet that was the last of them."

Hewey was doubtful. "Did you look in the bunkhouse?"

"It's all right. Needs some cleaning, but it'll do, I reckon. There's a big pile of trash beside it. I guess they were too lazy to do anything besides throw it out the door."

"They wouldn't have done that when C.C. was

around. Tomorrow we're goin' to Upton City to buy some stuff," Hewey said. "We best go by and say hello to your folks while we're close, let them know we're here."

"I reckon so," Tommy replied.

"Right now, I want both of us to make a little vuelta before dark. Just trot around, see what cattle you can find. I don't like it that we didn't see much comin' in here."

Tommy asked, "Somethin' bothering you?"

"Maybe," said Hewey. "Let's go see what we can find."

Hewey sent Tommy north, and after telling Spring their plans and promising to be back before dark, he headed mostly south, planning to circle around toward the west and then back to headquarters. Tommy had ridden the roan colt, which he had taken to calling Frog, for reasons he had not shared. Hewey rode the dun, Pincushion, who had done nothing but lazily follow the buggy for the last few days.

Cattle should have been coming to water at the dirt tank behind the house, so Hewey skirted around, searching for tracks. He found some, although not nearly as many as he felt he should.

He followed the fenceline for a couple miles, looking it over. Fences had always made Hewey sad, but he had grudgingly come to accept their necessity. Still, he longed for the days when the range was open and a man could ride wherever he pleased without finding a barbwire fence blocking his way.

There was a time not so long before when the buffalo and the Comanches still roamed this part of Texas, and the thought stirred something in Hewey. Years earlier, he had seen some of the last buffalo in Palo Duro Canyon while working for the JA Ranch. He had seen great piles of buffalo bones on the plains of Kansas, leftovers from the buffalo slaughter. That sight had put Hewey in a depressed mood that lasted for days.

But the days of the buffalo and the Comanches, and even the old open range ranches, were gone. C.C. Tarpley had despised fences as much as anyone, partly for the same reasons that troubled Hewey but even more for their cost. In time he was forced to relent. He kept a full-time fencing crew for over two years. Fortunately for Hewey, that had not been so many years ago. It appeared the ranch's fences were in good shape.

There were several windmills scattered around the ranch, although it had been so long since Hewey was on the place that he could not remember the exact location of them all. He remembered one about three or four miles west of the house and headed for it, hoping to jump some cattle along the way.

He began to run into a few scattered bunches of cattle, five here and ten there, but it still did not seem like enough for the miles he was covering.

He found the windmill, which was slowly

pumping a small stream of water into a large dirt tank. There were about twenty head of cattle, all cows with small calves at their sides, shaded up under some mesquite trees nearby. Meandering cattle trails came from several directions and converged at the tank. Hewey noted with some relief that all the trails had recent cattle tracks in them.

Hewey sat on Pincushion a couple of minutes, studying the cattle. When he nudged the dun into a walk and neared the cattle, they began drifting away, suspicious of the horse and rider.

The calves were unbranded, which did not surprise Hewey. He had expected that. Fat Gervin would not have gone to the trouble and expense of branding cattle he was planning to leave when the ranch sold.

Something had been troubling Hewey, although he had not been certain what it was until just then. The land contract had stated the cattle were Hereford and Hereford-Longhorn cross. While Hewey had a nostalgic sort of affinity for Longhorn cattle, he had come to respect the Hereford and other improved beef breeds. A Hereford calf at six months old weighed roughly twice what a Longhorn of the same age did, which equated to more money for the rancher. Hereford calves not only weighed more, but they also brought much more per pound than a Longhorn. A Hereford calf weighing twice as much might sell for three times the amount of its Longhorn cousin.

The Blessing

As foreman of the Circle W, Hewey had begun to look at cattle from the business side of things, whereas before he always left those matters to others. Cattle had been a source of employment, and often entertainment, nothing more.

What was troubling Hewey then, as he watched the cows and calves disappear into the low brush, was while the calves did show some Hereford influence, the only cows he had seen were straight Longhorn. He had not seen even a crossbred cow.

Hewey eased Pincushion into an easy trot, making a circle to the southeast that should end up back at the house.

"You look over these cattle," he told the dun horse. "Tell me what you think."

Pincushion twitched an ear in apparent acknowledgement but gave no further response. They passed several small bunches scattered along their route, but it still nagged Hewey that it just did not seem like enough cattle. But one thing was certain. He had not seen a single Hereford.

Tommy beat him back to headquarters, although not by much. Hewey asked his nephew what he had found.

"There's a windmill a few miles mostly north of here. There were quite a few pairs in a little draw close to it. Maybe sixty or eighty cows. Looked like most had calves. I probably passed that many more scattered here and there."

That made Hewey feel a little better on the numbers, at least. "What were they, the cows?"

Tommy thought a second, wondering what Hewey meant. "Oh," he said finally. "They were Longhorns. Calves looked like they were probably by a Hereford bull."

"All of them?" asked Hewey.

"All the calves?"

Hewey realized he was not getting his point across. "The cows. Were they all Longhorns? No Herefords? No crossbreds?"

Tommy closed one eye, thinking back. "Nope. Don't believe so. Just Longhorns. Why?"

"I think that fat son of a bitch is up to somethin'."

As they were preparing to leave for Upton City the next morning, Hewey looked up to find a lone rider trotting down the dim trail that led to the headquarters from the main road. Tommy walked up, and they both studied the visitor as he grew closer.

Tommy smiled and Hewey cursed lightly as recognition struck them both. Riding a neat little black horse that Hewey knew had belonged to Morgan Jenkins only a few days earlier was Enrique Rodriguez. The boy was grinning joyfully as he pulled up in front of them.

"Enrique, what in the hell are you doin' here?" Hewey demanded. "I told you to stay back on the

Circle W."

"Once you left, Mister Hooey, my tio, he turned into a terrible patron. Mean, work me like a dog, call me bad names," Enrique said earnestly. "I was forced to steal a horse and run away from home."

Hewey glared at the teenage boy for a few seconds. It was quickly all too much for Enrique, who broke out laughing. Tommy soon joined him. Hewey shook his head, disgusted with them both, although the corners of his mouth quivered and threatened to rise.

"Okay, esto es la verdad," Enrique was still smiling at his own joke. "I want to come with you, an' you say no. Once you gone, Aparicio starts to worry. He say sometimes you get yourself in trouble, that you can't help it. So he tell me to come check on you. So, aqui estoy."

Hewey dismissed the notion that he would get himself into trouble. He wasn't even sure where Aparicio got that ridiculous idea. However, he was aware that he needed more help on the place. "Did Aparicio give you that horse?"

Enrique shook his head sadly. "No, my tio, he sell me this horse for twenty dollars, almost all I had."

Hewey sighed. "Put your stuff in the bunkhouse. Tommy'll show you."

They left Enrique at the ranch with orders to prowl the pastures, doctor screwworm cases and look over any windmills he found. Hewey disliked leaving the boy alone, but he felt like he should go visit Walter and Eve. As for Tommy, there was no choice. He had to go. Hewey knew Eve would take it out on him if he showed up there without her son.

It took a couple hours to reach Walter and Eve's stock farm. There was a large flock of wool sheep grazing near the road. Walter had been in the sheep business for years, but it still rankled Hewey. His brother had once been a top hand, one of the best cowboys around. He ran the Two Cs for C.C. Tarpley for a time. Now he was a farmer who raised sheep. Hewey could not decide which was worse.

They found Walter in a small cotton field, holding the wooden handles of a mule-drawn cultivator. The dirt recently turned over by the plow looked hard and dry, unwelcoming to the struggling cotton plants that grew out of it. This land had never been meant to feel the bite of a plow, as far as Hewey was concerned.

Walter saw them and waited at the end of a row. He was tall and thin, clad in overalls and leather work shoes. Sweat ran down his face in rivulets, leaving streaks down Walter's dusty cheeks.

Tommy dismounted and walked to his father. Walter was grinning as his son approached. Tommy held out a hand. Walter grabbed it, then jerked his son forward and into a long hug. Tommy was momentarily surprised, but then his body softened as he returned the embrace.

Finally, Walter drew back, new streaks running down his dusty face. "It's been too long. I'm glad to see you." He looked up at Hewey and Spring. "All of you."

Walter walked to the buggy and reached up to shake his brother's hand. A handshake sufficed for them, although it was a long one.

"Hello, Walter," Spring said warmly. "We've missed you."

Hewey looked around at the place, which was too big to see across anymore. Over the years Walter had slowly bought the land surrounding his original farm. He now owned several sections, much of it in grass but some in farmland. "You ain't still tryin' to handle all this on your own, are you? Looks like you need a full-time hand out here. Maybe two or three."

Walter nodded his agreement. "I do need help, that's for sure. But I can't hardly afford to pay wages, not full-time, at least. Me and Eve, we were broke when we started and seems like maybe we always will be. The farm got bigger, but somehow it still pays about the same."

"Brother, that's 'cause the land and the Lord will not bless a man who rapes the earth with those infernal plows." Hewey pointed at the plow sitting behind the idle team of mules.

Walter eyed his brother skeptically. They argued the farming point before. "The Lord? When did you get close enough to the Lord to know his designs?"

John Bradshaw

Hewey grinned down. "Me and the Lord been close for a long time. We just wasn't always that public about it."

Walter turned toward his plow, smiling. "Y'all go on up to the house. Eve's around somewhere."

Hewey had faced many a chilly reception from his sister-in-law in years past, but he felt reasonably safe this time. He could not figure out what she could be mad at him about now. Even so, he let Spring and Tommy lead the way into the house, giving him quick access to the door if need be.

Eve was cheerful, although most of it was directed at Tommy and Spring. She looked appraisingly up and down Spring's frame, and a faint frown crossed her face for just a second. She pulled out a kitchen chair for Spring, then cast a disapproving look at Hewey, who was holding firm near the door. "Dern it, Hewey, I ain't going to bite you, not this time." Eve surprised him then by stepping close and giving him a small hug. "I'm glad you're back. So is Walter."

She turned her gaze to her son, who was rummaging through the kitchen in search of something to eat. "Tommy, there's a yellow rooster out there missing about half its feathers. I want you to catch him. It's been a long time since I had family in my kitchen. We'll celebrate."

Tommy found some leftover biscuits, took two and headed outside. Eve watched him go, a satisfied smile on her face. "I see he's still hungry all the time."

The Blessing

Hewey snorted. "I'm gonna have to take out a loan just to feed him. He earns thirty a month, but it costs me that much or more to keep him fed."

"I remember." Eve smiled, and Hewey relaxed just a little bit.

"Where is Cotton?" asked Spring.

"Moved to Midland. He got a better job in another garage. Those automobiles are all he thinks about, seems like. But he's good at it, and it suits him. He was here a few weeks ago, said a man in some city invented an electric icebox. Keeps your food cold, so it don't spoil so soon. Cotton said one day every home will have one. Can you imagine?"

Neither Hewey nor Spring could imagine such a thing and said so. "Heck, it won't matter none," Hewey said. "Ain't no way you'd ever get electricity way out here."

Eve said, mostly to Spring, "Cotton brought a girl out here last time. They didn't say, but I got the feelin' they might be thinking about a wedding."

That was enough women's talk for Hewey, and he stood abruptly. "I best go make sure Tommy don't need any help with that rooster."

He found Walter at the barn, removing the harness from the mules. Hewey said, "I hear you had somethin' to do with those folks buyin' me the ranch."

Walter shook his head. "Not much, really, but I did talk to them. Didn't believe it at first, that somebody would buy a ranch and just give it to *you*."

"I hope you ain't been tellin' that story around. I'd just as soon folks thought I struck it rich somehow, or I saved my wages all these years and just bought it outright."

"We haven't told a soul, but I guarantee you there ain't a big-enough fool in Upton County to believe you saved up your wages and bought it. Everyone knows you got holes in your pockets."

Hewey grew serious. "I still don't know how to feel about this. I never took charity in my whole life, except a couple times when I was hurt. I just don't feel right about it."

"Dammit, Hewey. It's not charity. I know enough about the situation to understand that. You saved that man's life and then gave him nearly everything you had. If those folks want to pay you back now, all these years later, then let 'em. You don't have to be ashamed of it."

Hewey was silent. He had been feeling guilty, and maybe even a little ashamed. He did not care much for either.

Walter said, "You have a chance here to own land, and a hell of a lot of it, free and clear. I been fightin' my whole life for the same thing. Don't you piss it away because you've got a guilty conscience over somethin' you had no control of."

Hewey blinked. Walter rarely spoke to him this way. Eve maybe, but not Walter. But his brother was right, and deep down he knew it.

"Hewey, you have a chance here to have something permanent. Something to put your name on. Something to hand down."

"Hand down to who?" Hewey asked quietly, meeting his brother's eyes.

Walter did not reply. He had no answer for that one.

Chapter Six

Hewey and Spring left Walter's place headed cross country toward Alvin Lawdermilk's ranch. Spring had spent several years living there and teaching at the country school the Lawdermilk family provided for children in the area. The couple had never been blessed with children of their own, so they built a small school so that children would always be nearby.

It was summertime, so the school was quiet when they arrived. The Lawdermilk family always kept a menagerie of livestock around the headquarters. Hewey was forced to slow the buggy for an insolent billy goat that refused to yield the right of way, and the screeching guinea hens told everyone that strangers had arrived.

Alvin sat in the shade near a corral, watching a man try to harness a young bronc. Three more horses stood tied outside the corral, waiting their turn. Alvin looked up when the guineas began their racket, and he eased toward the house. Hewey noted that his friend moved slower than the last time they had seen each other. "Dern, but Alvin's gettin' old," he told Spring. She gave him a look that told him Alvin might not be the only one. Hewey knew what she meant without being told.

"Hell, Alvin's older than me."

Spring patted him on the knee. "I know it, and you haven't aged a bit," she said. "Not since this morning, at least."

Alvin stopped several feet away to appraise the gray team pulling the wagon. "Goodness," he said. "But that just might be the best-looking team I ever saw. Reckon where a feller could get horses like that?"

Like most good horsemen, Alvin could recognize a horse as well as he recognized people, maybe better. He knew he had raised those grays.

Smiling, Spring said, "These came from an old man out near the Pecos River. He raises good horses, but he's a typical horse trader. You've got to watch him."

"That's no joke," said Cora Lawdermilk, who had just stepped out onto the porch and was shading her eyes with her hand. A broad smile showed beneath the hand. She had wanted desperately for Spring to marry Hewey, but then it had saddened her fiercely when Spring moved away immediately after the wedding. They had not seen each other in three years.

Alvin helped Spring step down from the buggy, and Hewey followed her. The women hugged each other, both crying joyful tears. Hewey and Alvin shook hands, then eyed their wives suspiciously.

"How is Mrs. Faversham?" Spring asked Cora, looking around. Old Lady Faversham was Cora's mother, a large woman with a difficult personality. She had lived with Cora and Alvin for many years and made her son-in-law miserable every one of them. She was known to distrust all men, footloose cowboys especially and Hewey Calloway most of all. She had done all she could to prevent the courtship and subsequent marriage between Hewey and Spring.

"Mother passed away last November," Cora said somberly.

"Oh, Cora, I'm so sorry," Spring said. She really was sorry for Cora, but personally she would not miss Mrs. Faversham.

"That's just awful," Hewey added.

"Tragic," agreed Alvin.

Frightened by the looks from their wives, Hewey and Alvin retreated toward the corrals. Alvin's longtime employee Julio Valdez was working with a young bronc in the smaller of the corrals, and they watched him.

"Que pasa, Julio?" Hewey asked his old friend.

Julio continued to work with the bronc, although he smiled at Hewey. "Same old things, my friend. You come back here to work with us?"

Hewey had many times over the years worked for Alvin Lawdermilk, mostly helping to break young horses and mules.

"No, not exactly," said Hewey.

Alvin looked at him curiously, so Hewey explained. "I did want to talk to you about you maybe sending us some broncs, if you've got any extra you and Julio can't get to. I thought we might make some kind of deal. I need using horses, but right now I hate to spend the money buying any. Hell, it's not that I hate to spend the money. I ain't got the money."

Alvin nodded. A little twinkle formed in his eye, but he caught himself before a smile showed. Hewey was his good friend, but business was business and Alvin smelled a good deal. Also, the fact was that he and Julio were not keeping up with all the young horses he owned. They had not for a long time. Every year they got older, but the broncs stayed the same.

He asked Hewey who he had working for him on the ranch. Hewey told him of Enrique's skill with a horse. Tommy had ridden horses for Alvin for many years, so no explanation was necessary there.

A veteran horse trader, Alvin began telling Hewey how the horse market had dropped off due to the rise in automobile popularity. "You heard of these new tractors?" he asked Hewey.

Hewey had heard of them, but he felt fortunate to have not seen one in person. He told Alvin so.

"I don't know, Hewey, I been hearin' that before long, ever' farmer in the country will have one to plow his fields, and they won't even need no more work horses."

"Shoot, there ain't no way," Hewey said. "The way I heard it, those tractors are so weak and slow a feller can't get nothin' done with one."

"I hope that's right, but it's makin' me nervous. I

don't know what's to become of the market for work horses and mules. I might be out of business altogether if I ain't careful," Alvin said, "But, I guess I might could send you some broncs, but I'd be doin' it more as a favor than as a wise business decision."

Hewey eyed the older man skeptically, knowing this was not Alvin's first horse trade. Alvin asked him, "What are you thinking?"

Hewey scratched his chin. "You send us ten, maybe even twenty head at a time. We'll break 'em and keep them a couple months at whatever the goin' rate is anymore. I don't even know what that is, but I bet you do. After a couple months we'll trade them out and take another bunch, if you got 'em."

That was not a bad deal, considering who would be handling the horses, and Alvin knew it. But it was not what he had in mind. "Times are changing, Hewey. Folks are gettin' soft. They don't want some bronc with sixty days on him, just a little bit of the rough knocked off. Maybe I can sell that kind to some ranch needin' some more usin' horses, but not these farmers or the general public. They want somethin' gentler, easier to handle. I don't know what the world is comin' to, I tell you."

Hewey waited, not knowing where this was going. Alvin looked off into the distance with a wistful look, legitimately saddened by the state of the world. "Let's slip off behind the barn. I got a bottle hid behind that big mesquite tree."

The Blessing

Alvin had always been known to drink often, and occasionally to excess. Cora had never held with much drinking, and his late mother-in-law was vocal in her disapproval, so Alvin had always kept bottles hidden across his ranch.

The last Hewey had heard, Alvin had given up drinking. Alvin had set off walking toward his stash with a single-minded purpose. Following, Hewey said, "I thought you give up drinkin'."

Alvin continued in his determined walk and did not look back as he answered. "I did for a spell, but I quit that foolishness." He had reached a large, forked mesquite tree, hidden from view of the house by the big wooden horse barn. A large, flat white rock leaned against the base of the tree. Alvin grabbed the top of the rock, cautiously leaned it over, and peered into the shadow between the rock and tree.

"You got to be careful. Once there was a little rattlesnake in there coiled up next to my medicine." He removed a glass bottle that contained an amber liquid. Alvin removed the cork and took a long, obviously satisfying pull, then handed the bottle to Hewey, who took a smaller drink. The label had worn off, if there had ever been one, but it was not bottom-shelf liquor and Hewey knew it. Alvin always sprang for the good stuff.

Alvin had not finished his explanation of why he had gone back to drinking. "You know, everyone was always preachin' at me about drinkin', so I done some studying on it myself. Now, I admit the Bible does speak against drunkenness. But there's all sorts of talk about drinkin'. Hell, Jesus himself turned water to wine."

Alvin took the bottle from Hewey and had another pull. "Here's my favorite. Ecclesiastes says to eat your food with gladness and drink your wine with a joyful heart, for God has already approved what you do."

Pointing the bottle at Hewey, Alvin said, "Who am I to argue with the Lord?"

No argument came to mind for Hewey, so he took another drink himself. Alvin had another pull, then stashed the bottle behind the rock. He rubbed his hands together. "All right. Now I can think. I ain't kiddin' about people wantin' a different kind of horse, Hewey. I know you can ride a rough one as good as anyone, or could." He looked down at Hewey's leg.

"Still can, damn it," Hewey said.

"Sure. Sure. But I'm tellin' you, that ain't the way it's goin' anymore. You need to think about this. As good as you are with a horse, you could do somethin' with it. There's money to be made on it, I guarantee you."

Hewey's brow was furrowed in thought. "Those boys I got workin' for me are good with horses. We'll work at it, see what we can do."

"That's all I'm askin'," said Alvin, getting down to business. "Now, I got twenty-four head of nice four-year-olds. Raised them all myself. Probably should've been started last year, but we never got around to 'em. They're halter broke and been handled just a little. Won't be no trouble for y'all."

"They geldings?" asked Hewey.

"Well hell yes, they're geldings. This is Texas. I know you boys won't ride mares."

Hewey held up a hand to calm his friend. "Okay, I'm just checkin'. What's the pay?"

"I don't want to pay you. I want to partner on 'em. I want you to take them and ride them for six months. You feed them and take good care of them. Then we'll sell them, and you get a third of the money."

"Half the money," countered Hewey.

Alvin frowned and had to go back to his bottle to think about it. A little refreshment had always helped him think more clearly. "You keep them for a year and you can have half."

Smiling, Hewey stuck out his hand. "Deal," he said. "But you'll have to sell them. You're the horse trader."

Alvin smiled. *I might be*, he thought. He had just outtraded Hewey Calloway.

Every ranch of a certain size needed a name, Hewey knew, and more importantly, a brand. He had given it much thought but could not decide what to call the place. He felt like naming it after his wife, but nothing seemed fitting. There was not a spring to be found. There were some windmills and dirt tanks, but that did not make sense.

Spring had no specific ideas but did tell him he was making it too difficult. "Just keep it simple," she told him one evening. "You're going to hurt yourself with all this thinking."

So, in the end he settled for something simple, the H-C, or H bar C. Everyone would assume the H stood for Hewey and the C for Calloway, he knew, but they would be partly wrong. The H stood for Henderson. Hewey figured if the Hendersons gave him a ranch then he ought to name it after them, even if quietly.

After all the difficulty making the decision on the name, Hewey found it mattered very little. Neither he nor Spring was much concerned with the name, and even if they had been, they did not have the spare money to put up a sign anywhere.

The main reason had been that he needed a brand, and quickly. The calves would soon need branded, and every cow on the place needed his brand, as well. They all carried the Two Cs brand. Cattle theft had become much less common over the last couple decades, but Hewey would not put it past Fat Gervin to pay a couple conscienceless cowpunchers to slip over and drive a few cows through a gate.

Chapter Seven

Tommy, Enrique and Hewey spent the next two weeks horseback, making drives and gathering all the cattle they could find. The ranch was not so big that they really needed a chuckwagon, and Hewey did not own a chuckwagon anyway. So, they stayed at the headquarters and rode out early and returned late, particularly when they were working in the areas farthest from headquarters.

Spring rode with them every two or three days. She had begun riding out with Hewey occasionally while they lived near Alpine. Hewey knew she was lonely being alone at the house all day, and she was good help, which they needed. Plus, when she came along, Tommy and Enrique kept their foolishness to a minimum.

Every afternoon or evening they worked with Alvin Lawdermilk's broncs. The young horses, for the most part, had good sense and were easy enough to get started. Hewey took it as a testament to their good bloodlines, but also to the handling they had received from Alvin and Julio. After only a couple rides in the corral, Tommy and Enrique began to use the young horses on the drive each day. This caused some excitement and fun for everyone, but Tommy and Enrique were both young and talented enough that they handled it in stride.

Hewey had noticed that Enrique always stepped off his horse on the right side, rather than the left as most everyone else did. Hewey had, of course, seen this done before and had even done it himself on occasion. But Enrique did it every time. Curious, Hewey asked the boy about the habit one day as they ate a cold lunch in the shade of a small mesquite tree.

"My papá, he taught me that long ago, when I was a little boy. It was what he did, so I do the same."

"Yeah, but what for? Why'd your papa do it?" asked Hewey, genuinely curious. The three of them often talked of horses and of horse training. It was their favorite topic. Usually, it was Enrique and Tommy asking the questions, but Hewey was not so set in his ways that he would not consider changing them if there were good reason.

Enrique pondered the question. Finally, he said, "Papá, he said it's good for the horse. Makes him mansito. He also say it's good for the saddle. You always step just in the left stirrup, it gets stretched, makes it longer. You step off the other side, it gets stretched too. This way, they stay the same."

Both Hewey and Tommy thought about that. It made sense, although neither had ever thought about it before.

After a minute, Tommy asked, "Where's your pa now?"

Enrique gazed off into the distance, then said, "El

murio. When I was twelve years old a horse fell on my papá. It hurt something inside him. Two days later, he went to be with my mamá."

"Damn," said Tommy. "You lost both your parents?"

"Si."

"What happened to your mother?" asked Tommy.

"She was sick. I do not know what from," said Enrique. "I was very small."

Hewey asked, "Who raised you after your pa died?"

"I stay with my older sister for a while, but she has a family of her own. So many kids there was not so much room for me there. When I was thirteen, I go to work for a rancho at a place called Potrero del Llano. Few years later, I come to Texas to work for my tio, and you, Mister Hooey."

Hewey poked the bare ground with a stick. Enrique's story made him sad. He and Walter had lost both their parents, and there had been some gaunt times afterward. "Life ain't always fair, is it?" he asked Enrique.

"No, Mister Hooey, it is not. For some it is very bad. Pero, for some of us there is much luck. We are chosen to be vaqueros." He pointed at their horses standing hipshot in the shade, then at the ranchland beyond. "We get to do this ever' day."

Hewey smiled faintly, admiring the boy's outlook. Some people often saw the good over the bad, even when their own circumstances were difficult. There was a time Hewey had been that way, and he wished he could go back.

"I tell you what, son," Hewey said quietly, staring at the ground. "You got a place here, long as you want it."

Each day they gathered a couple sections or so, depending on the terrain. They drove them to a prearranged spot where they held them up and counted them. Hewey had considered trying to count the cattle without gathering them, but he just could not figure out an accurate way to do it.

At the end of each day, they pushed the cattle that had been counted far away from the direction of the next day's drive in an attempt to only gather uncounted animals the following day. The method seemed to be working well, although Hewey knew it was not entirely accurate.

He disliked the idea of gathering the cattle without going ahead and branding the calves, and maybe the cows also, but he wanted to get an idea of what he was working with. Also, he simply did not have the manpower.

The sun was hot on their backs as all three rode across the pasture, headed home after a long day. They were following a narrow cattle trail that wound through the grass. Hewey, in the lead, saw the rattlesnake in a shady spot beside the trail just as his horse passed it. Tommy, a few feet behind Hewey, saw the snake and pulled his horse to a stop. Hewey turned his horse, and Enrique joined them. All three sat looking down at the snake, which had coiled its body, head raised, and begun to rattle quietly.

Three men and three horses stared down at the snake. Its rattling grew slightly louder, but it had yet to reach full volume. The horses were tired and had not been startled by the snake, so all three were relatively unconcerned with it.

Tommy said, "You know, every time there's a rattlesnake in those dime novels, the horse runs away or bucks off the feller right on top of the snake. I never seen a horse that much cared about a rattlesnake. These sure don't, and none of them are exactly gentle."

Enrique did not know what Tommy meant by dime novel. Hewey looked up from the snake and said, "That's because them fellers that write books don't know nothin' about horses. Or snakes."

Tommy nodded. Sounded right to him.

Over the last few days they had found two cattle, one a cow and the other a small calf, with fresh snakebites. The cow's leg was swollen and sore to the point they had to let her drop out of the drive because she traveled so slowly. The calf had been bitten on the nose, likely a wound of curiosity. It would live, but it would suffer for a while before it healed completely. Although Hewey had never been a fan of rattlesnakes, he was in a particularly foul mood with them just then.

"Tommy, hunt around and find a stick to kill it with."

"I'll double up my rope and hit it with that," Tommy replied.

"No, don't do that. I heard of a feller one time did that. A fang broke off in the rope and he didn't know it. When he coiled up his rope that fang stuck in his hand, still had some venom in it. Damned near killed him."

Tommy was not sure he believed the story, but then again he wasn't sure he did not. He began looking around for a piece of mesquite long enough to safely dispatch a snake. The portion of the ranch they were in was mostly grass with a few low mesquites and the occasional catclaw. There were not many options as far as snake-killing tree branches went.

Enrique stepped off his horse, started to drop the reins, then thought better of it. The colt only had a few days on it and looked as if it might abandon him. He wisely tied it to a low mesquite. "I'll show you how we kill the vibora de cascabel in Mexico."

Weaponless, he began walking toward the snake. Hewey realized what he was planning and said, "Don't do that, Enrique. I've seen your uncle do it, and I can't figure how he didn't get bit."

"No pasa nada," Enrique said.

Hewey shook his head. "It'll be a big deal if that snake bites you."

The Blessing

Tommy returned with a slender mesquite branch about four feet long, which was about a foot longer than the snake. He looked at Enrique, curious. He didn't know what his friend was planning.

"Let me borrow your stick, Tomas."

Tommy handed the stick to Enrique. The snake's rattle grew louder as he neared it. Enrique tried to pin the snake's head with the stick, but the snake moved quickly, then struck at the branch.

"Calmate, amigo," he said soothingly. "No me muerdas."

Not at all soothed, the snake struck again. When it pulled its head back into the coil, Enrique was able to get the stick over the snake's head and pin it to the ground. The snake twisted the length of its body, spinning wildly in an effort to free itself, but the stick held the head still.

Quickly Enrique reached down with his left hand and grabbed the snake just behind the head, gripping it tightly. Satisfied, he released the stick and picked up the snake.

Tommy was astonished. He had lived his life around rattlesnakes but had never seen anyone pick up a live one. "Boy, that's somethin'," he said, grinning. "But what are you gonna do now?"

Still on his horse, Hewey said, "He's gonna get bit if he ain't careful."

Enrique flashed a smile at Hewey. "It's okay, Mister Hooey. I did this many times in Mexico." He paused, thinking. "Well, maybeso one time."

"Oh, hell," said Hewey in exasperation. "Snakes can't hardly bite through your boots or chaps. I had a big diamondback strike the top of my boot one time down by Ozona. It about scared me to death, but it didn't go through. But when you start foolin' around like that, pickin' them up with your hands, you're liable to get bit."

Enrique just grinned, brimming with youthful confidence, then he walked several steps farther away, putting some distance between himself and Tommy. He reached down and grabbed the big snake by the tail, just above the rattle. "It's just like popping a whip," he said.

He was still for a few seconds, perhaps thinking it over. Hewey saw some of the confidence leave Enrique, as if the boy was not quite certain of what he was about to do but was steeling himself for it. He did not want to back down at this point, in front of Hewey and Tommy. Hewey said, "You don't have to do it, Enrique. Just kill it with the stick."

But he did have to continue. Hewey knew it. Tommy knew it, and Enrique certainly knew it. Machismo was as ingrained in him as much as his love for horses. In a quick series of movements, Enrique released the snake's head, letting it dangle by the tail, which he held in his right hand. His hand was close to waist height, so the snake's head almost touched the ground.

The Blessing

With a fast, fluid motion he raised his hand to shoulder height, then forward and slightly down, finally popping it backward, just as if he were popping a bullwhip. There was no sound, but the snake went limp. Enrique held it high, and they could all see the head was gone. The skin was torn and jagged just behind where the snake's head had been a moment earlier, some flesh and bone showing underneath.

Enrique beamed, then began laughing, from joy but also relief. Hewey smiled slightly, shaking his head. It was a neat trick. Dumb, but impressive.

Tommy walked the few steps over to Enrique and examined the snake. "What in the hell? Why does the head pop off?"

"Magic," Enrique said seriously.

Tommy's eyes narrowed as he studied Enrique, who remained silent. Tommy looked at Hewey. "Why?"

Hewey said, "I thought about it a lot after I saw it done the first time. I guess it just snaps off when the snake pops like a whip. But hell, I don't know."

"Magic," insisted Enrique.

"You've seen this before?" Tommy asked Hewey.

"A few times. Aparicio could do it. There was a feller named Jaime killed a few that way when me and Snort went to Mexico back when you was still a kid."

Tommy began hunting around on the ground, looking for the snake's head. He wanted to see what it looked like after being whipped off the body, but he never found it.

The snake, still dangling from Enrique's hand, began to move as its muscles contracted. It curled up, almost as if it were going to strike Enrique.

Watching, Tommy said, "That always gave me the willies. I don't see how they can move so much without their heads."

"We killed a big cascabel in Mexico a few years ago," Enrique told him. "We skinned it, took out its guts and then cooked the whole snake over a fire. There was nothing left but meat and bones, but it kept jumping off the fire. Finally we had to put a big rock on it to hold it down."

As an accomplished teller of tall tales, Hewey recognized one and suppressed a grin. Tommy eyed Enrique, uncertain. "You're joshin' me again."

"No, esto es la verdad. Finally, we got the snake cooked and cut it into pieces, maybe this long." Enrique held his thumb and forefinger about three inches apart. "My abuelo, he dumped those pieces on a table so everybody could take some. Those little pieces of snake, they all started moving around, going this way and that way. Pretty soon, they put themselves back together into the big snake."

Hewey began to laugh, and Enrique burst into a fit of giggles.

"Now I know you're full of bull," said Tommy, laughing also. He moved as if to grab Enrique, who raised the snake between them. "Cuidado, amigo, or I will be forced to sic my snake on you."

Still smiling, Enrique took a short, thin knife from his belt and slit the snake down the underside. He left the skin covering the snake but was still able to easily remove the guts. He then coiled it up and walked to his horse. The sorrel bronc rolled its nose and looked at Enrique and the snake warily, but a couple soothing words in Spanish calmed it. Using the saddle strings, he tied the snake to his saddle.

Tommy had watched him. "What you gonna do with it now?"

"I will make some jerky," replied Enrique. "It's easy. You'll see. Put a little salt, then hang it in the sun for a few days. You'll like it."

Tommy was not too sure he *would* like it. "Well, you better make sure your knots are tight, else it might get loose, jump off your horse and slither away."

Hewey and Enrique looked at each other sadly, and Hewey shook his head side to side. Tommy saw the exchange and asked, "What?"

Looking at his nephew seriously, Hewey said, "Tommy, you're a good boy. You got lots of talents. But you just ain't funny."

Hewey's discouragement over the cattle quality increased each day, and his anger and irritability grew along with it. The sales contract had said there were approximately five hundred cows on the ranch. It also stated those cows were Hereford or Hereford-Longhorn crosses. Hewey and his small crew had found a few Herefords and a few more crossbreds, but he had noticed that all of those had been particularly wild, the kind that were often difficult to gather and might have been missed.

Most of the cows were older Longhorns, a breed that stirred Hewey's sentimental nature due to its long history in Texas. He had spent his life with the Longhorn, which was an old friend and occasional adversary. However, his growing business nature brought with it a new perspective.

Tommy and Enrique knew something was bothering Hewey more and more as the days went by, although he was not talking about it with them. One afternoon as they trotted back toward headquarters, Tommy broached the subject. "Somethin' botherin' you, Uncle Hewey?"

Hewey had been deep in thought and was momentarily startled by the question. Tommy was young, Enrique even younger, and he had not wanted to burden them with his troubles. He talked about it to Spring every evening, but not to the boys. "Oh, I'm sure it's nothin'," he said finally.

Tommy and Enrique exchanged glances. Enrique chose to remain silent. It was not his place, or way, to ask questions. Tommy was not burdened by either. "Come on, Uncle Hewey. Ain't but three of us here. You might as well tell us what's eatin' on you."

Hewey trotted on without responding. Frustrated, Tommy said more than was common for him. "Dern it, Uncle Hewey! My whole life I wanted to be like you, and it wasn't never because you were some bigtime rancher. It was because everybody talked about what a good cowboy you were, but mostly because you were always so fun to be around. Don't lose that, Uncle Hewey. I'm askin' you."

Enrique quietly slowed his horse, putting some distance between himself and the two Calloways. Things were developing into something he wanted no part of, although he stayed within easy earshot. It might be too good to miss.

Still trotting along in the lead, Hewey straightened his shoulders and stretched his back, looking upward in thought. He checked his horse, slowing to a walk and then stopping altogether. He turned and faced them. Enrique had stopped twenty feet back.

Hewey looked at both of them. He knew they were both there with him out of loyalty. It bothered him that he had shut them out, even though he had believed it had been for their own good. "Hell, boys, I'm sorry. I just didn't want to trouble you with my problems."

He told them about the contract and how the cattle did not match the description. Knowing the characters, Tommy caught on quickly. "So you think Fat Gervin sorted off the nice cattle and left you with the culls?"

"Yeah, I'm beginnin' to think Fat did somethin' like that," Hewey said. "But don't you be callin' him

Fat. You better call him Mister Gervin. Your folks might still have a note at his bank. You don't want him takin' it out on them if he hears you been callin' him that."

Tommy said, "My folks got that note paid off, and I don't think they'll ever borrow money from Fat again."

Hewey shook his head. "Still, it'd be best if you don't call him Fat."

Enrique was curious. "Who is this Senor Fat?"

"Oh, hell," said Hewey, exasperated. "It's like runnin' a nursery school around here."

Spring continued to ride with them two or three times per week. The four of them left headquarters at dawn one morning, trotting southwest. Spring rode Biscuit. Tommy, Enrique and Hewey all rode Lawdermilk horses, none of which had more than thirty rides on them. Spring constantly fussed at Hewey about riding the broncs, but he just got so *bored* riding older horses.

They had only gone a mile or two when they heard unusual sounds ahead. They cleared a small mesquite thicket and saw two feral hogs rooting in the brush beyond. Feral hogs were common to the south and east. Twenty years earlier none were found in Upton County, but the destructive creatures were beginning to show up in the area.

The Blessing

In years past, Hewey felt ambivalence toward the long-haired, long-tusked feral hogs. Now, with the responsibility of land ownership thrust upon him, he saw with new eyes what the pigs could do to the landscape. They rooted up good grass, destroyed dirt tanks and occasionally even tore up fences. He knew they played hell with crops, but that was the farmers' business.

The four riders reined to a stop in silence, horses and riders all studying the feral hogs. The pigs began easing away, but they were not yet frightened and thus moved slowly. Taking his time so he would not startle the pigs, Hewey reached down with his right hand and untied his rope from where it hung on his saddle. Tommy and Enrique saw his intent. Grinning, they followed his lead.

Spring saw as well. She was not grinning. "Hewey, don't you do it."

Hewey just looked at his wife and winked, then quietly built a small loop. He held the coils of his rope in his left hand, loop in the right. He held his reins in both hands because his bronc was too green to ride one-handed. He would have to plow rein it up behind the hog, then bring up his rope once the horse was lined out. No problem. They did it all the time on cattle.

The feral hogs were young, neither weighing more than fifty or sixty pounds. Without a word, Hewey kicked his sorrel bronc into a lope, then into a run, headed toward the hogs.

Tommy and Enrique followed behind, both whooping with pure glee. Spring sat still on Biscuit, slightly amused, slightly angry. "Lord help us," she said to Biscuit.

Things might have been different had they jumped the wild hogs later in the day, after the fresh was knocked off their horses. The horses might have been tired enough not to be frisky, and they might have behaved better.

Enrique's bay colt had traveled with a hump in its back most of the morning. It was still tight when Enrique kicked it into a run. They had only gone fifty feet when a large catclaw bush blocked their path.

Enrique assumed the bay would go around the bush. Most young horses would have. There was plenty of room. Instead, the bay jumped the catclaw, which rose two feet out of the dry, sandy ground. The sudden and unexpected jump loosened Enrique in the saddle ever so slightly. The colt, being young and foolish, somehow frightened itself by jumping the catclaw. As soon as its front feet hit the ground it ducked its head and began bucking earnestly.

The landing had pushed Enrique forward in the saddle. When the bay dropped its head, it felt to Enrique like there was nothing in front of his saddle other than hard Upton County dirt. He never had a chance. He lasted three jumps and was thrown over the front end. The colt bucked for a hundred feet farther, then pulled up and snorted at the excitement taking place around it.

Tommy pursued the hog on the left, a red animal that ran surprisingly fast for the length of its legs. Still, Tommy's palomino colt had no trouble overtaking the smaller animal. As they closed the distance, Tommy began to lightly pull on his hackamore reins to slow his horse. He needed it to rate, to match its speed with that of the pig. Then Tommy would be able to throw his rope.

The palomino had never seen such excitement and had, in fact, never before seen a wild hog. Its young mind was overwhelmed. The horse felt an overload of fear, exhilaration and adrenaline. Tommy pulled harder on the reins, and the palomino ignored him. As they passed the terrified red pig, Tommy began to saw on the reins. The bronc felt the rawhide bosal bite into its nose, and it ran faster. Far behind, Enrique raised up off the ground in time to watch Tommy disappear over a sandhill, the yellow horse headed south as fast as its legs could carry them.

Intent on the black pig he had chosen, Hewey had not witnessed the two mishaps, although he did get the sense that he was suddenly alone in his chase.

The sorrel horse Hewey was riding was called Alvin. Cowboys often named horses after their previous owners, and Hewey just sort of thought Alvin was an amusing name for a horse. Alvin had been coming along nicely, perhaps showing more natural good sense than his namesake. Hewey had used him quite a bit and had even roped several wormy cattle on him. Alvin had always been cool under pressure, but then again no one had ever asked him to pursue a feral hog.

A decade or so earlier, Hewey had roped a feral hog down in the Hill Country. He had been mounted well that day, though, not on a raw bronc. He knew the feral hogs were fast and agile, but he also knew a horse could easily run one down. So, unlike Tommy, he had wisely held Alvin somewhat in check, easing up behind the black hog, rather than running full tilt.

Alvin had plenty of cow, which is what cowboys called a horse's natural instinct to work cattle. In Alvin's case, it worked just as well on feral hogs. When the pig darted one way and then the other, Alvin followed with little command from above. Hewey noticed this, and for a moment, he was proud of the little horse.

Alvin had rated, somewhat at least, several feet behind the pig. Feeling things were right, Hewey dropped the hackamore rein out of his right hand and brought up his rope. In his mind, he planned to rope the pig around the middle. He knew his rope might slip right off the pig's neck if there was not a leg in there to stop it from pulling free.

Intent on the pig, Hewey swung one time, planning to throw on the second or possibly the third swing. Alvin was watching the pig, Hewey was watching the pig, and the pig itself was too short to see over the low brush it barreled straight through. None of them saw the dry gully, not until it was too late.

Running water happens occasionally in West Texas. The infrequent rains often come in torrents, washing toward the low areas. Soon the land is dry again, gouged earth the only sign water had ever flowed there. This particular gully was wider than it was deep. At the center, it was only two or three feet lower than the land around it, but it was fully ten feet across, bank to bank.

The pig finally saw the wash, and it slowed almost imperceptibly. Hewey and Alvin saw the gully, but they did not see the pig slowing in their path.

Both horse and rider looked back at the pig. Hewey pulled the reins, but it was too late. Alvin stepped on the pig with his left front foot, almost causing him to fall. The pig squealed from pain or from fright, and then it ducked to the right.

Alvin and Hewey did not make the turn with the black pig, and instantly they were upon the dry gully. Alvin obviously thought he could make the jump. Hewey was fairly certain they could not. Without slowing, Alvin gathered his legs under him just before they went over the edge. He launched forward off his powerful hind legs.

It seemed to Hewey that they were suspended in the air momentarily. Alvin's forelegs were stretched forward, reaching for the far bank. Hewey held his reins and coils in his left hand, loop in his right.

Alvin might have cleared the wash had the pig not forced him to slow just before he made the jump. As it was, he came up short. Hewey saw the opposite bank coming toward them as they descended, and he knew the landing would be brutal.

The horse's head and neck cleared the bank, but Alvin's chest did not. The sandy dirt along the edge of the bank was crumbling and relatively soft, but even so the impact was sudden and jarring. Alvin's forward movement ceased in an instant.

There was no sandy bank in front of Hewey. His momentum continued. He was launched out of the saddle headfirst, skidding along the brushy ground for several feet until he was stopped abruptly by a thorny mesquite tree. He still had his rope in his hands, but he no longer had air in his lungs. The impact had knocked it out of him. For several seconds he felt as if he could not breathe at all, and then with a gasp, air rushed back into his aching chest.

Alvin rose to his feet in the bottom of the wash, unhurt yet uncertain. He climbed the far bank and trotted back toward the other horses. Hewey rolled over and sat on his butt, waiting for his breathing to return to normal. He wondered idly if he should feel foolish, attempting something so wild at his age. He decided he should not.

Spring came into sight from behind the brush, leading Alvin by a rein. Enrique followed behind her, silent, sheepish, again mounted on his bay horse.

Tommy was nowhere to be seen. Biscuit casually crossed the wash that had caused so much disaster minutes before, and Alvin calmly followed.

Pulling up near Hewey, Spring looked down at him. Her eyes twinkled, but she kept a straight face. She pitched the hackamore rein toward him. "If you children are done playing, I reckon we better get to work."

Chapter Eight

Screwworms were nothing new to Hewey, but over the years he had been noticing what seemed like an increase in the number of cases. The screwworm fly was larger than a housefly and had a bluish tint to its color. During the warm months the flies laid eggs in open wounds on livestock, wildlife and occasionally even people. The eggs hatched into small flesh-eating worms, much like maggots, and often the animal suffered a slow, torturous death.

Hewey, like all other cowboys, hated screwworms with vengeance. It troubled him to see livestock in his care suffering from a case of screwworms. It bothered him to see it in the wildlife, for there was nothing he could do to help them.

They also hated the screwworms for the distasteful task they presented to the cowboys. Infected animals had to be caught, almost always at the end of a rope. The worms were removed with a stick or whatever was handy that could be used to scrape them away, and finally the wound was treated with pine tar. It was a labor-intensive, nasty job, but one that could not be ignored.

Every day, Hewey, Tommy and Enrique kept watch for signs of wormy cattle. Usually, they quit what they were doing to immediately doctor anything they found. The process was much easier when there was more than one person. When alone, they were forced to rope the wormy animal, trip it, tie it down and then treat the wound.

When they were together, one of them roped the animal by the head and another by the hind legs. They then stretched the animal between two horses, which held it still. If there were only two of them, the man who had roped the head doctored the animal. If there were three, the man who had not roped was left to treat the wound.

Since the work was so unpleasant, there was much incentive to be one of those who caught the wormy animal and not the third man left to the doctoring.

Oftentimes they found newborn calves with screwworms in their navels. The raw navels drew the flies more than anything, it seemed. The small, quick calves were a challenge to catch, and then more often than not, the calf's mother would be less than appreciative of their efforts to save her offspring.

Late one hot morning, Hewey was trailing a small bunch of cattle, heading them in the general direction of a windmill where the drive was to converge. He noticed a calf, no more than a few days old, with screwworms around its navel. The calf was young and already becoming slightly weak from the worms. It dropped back to the rear of the herd, and soon Hewey was riding along just behind it.

The calf's mother, an older yellow-and-white Longhorn, was having an internal battle between her maternal instinct and her inclination toward self-preservation. She could not decide whether to stay with her calf or put some distance between herself and the horseman. Hewey watched the cow for a while, noting the yellow color, the thin, bony frame and long horns. She was certainly not one of the Herefords described in the sales contract. *I don't know if she's ever even seen a Hereford*, he thought crossly.

Quietly, Hewey took down his rope and tied the tail to his saddlehorn with a plaited rawhide horn knot. He was riding Biscuit, which he had been doing every so often to keep the old brown horse honest. He felt like Spring let Biscuit get away with too much, which required some occasional correction. Spring scoffed at the idea.

The calf was plodding along just in front of Biscuit, making an easy shot. Hewey took one quick swing, then threw his rope before the calf had time to move away.

The calf woke from its tired stupor when it felt the rope pull tight around its neck. It was small enough that Hewey did not bother to trip it with his horse. He pulled a short tie string from his saddle, ran down the rope and flanked the calf. Biscuit held the rope tight while Hewey quickly tied three of its legs together. When the calf was secure, Hewey walked back to his horse, casually took hold of one of the bridle reins and stepped Biscuit forward, giving the calf some slack. He untied the tail of the rope from the saddlehorn.

He took the can of pine tar from his saddlebags, then hunted around on the ground and found a stick suitable for the job. He removed the rope from the calf's neck, then began flicking away worms from the calf's navel with the stick. The wound made by the worms was not too severe, but Hewey reflected that it would have been in another few days, maybe less.

Still, the stink of the worms and the decaying flesh made his eyes water, and he stifled a gag. Years before he had wondered if he would ever get used to the smell. It had not happened yet.

When he had all the worms scraped away, Hewey opened his can of pine tar with his pocketknife. It always amazed him that the can could be so difficult to open yet could still somehow leak in his saddlebags. He poured a generous amount of the foul pine tar on the wound, then smeared it around with his stick.

The calf began to struggle and then to bawl for its mother. Hewey had been keeping an eye on the cow, which had been watching from a respectful distance, at least up until the calf began to bawl. The sound was more than she could bear. The cow came at a trot, head down and blowing snot. Hewey was done with the calf, and he began trying to untie its legs. The calf strained and kicked, which slowed the untying.

Biscuit, not for the first time, came to Hewey's aid. The brown horse saw the cow coming and moved up to meet her. The horse pinned its ears and jumped in front of the cow, then sidestepped as she tried to go around him. Hewey finally got the string loose and stood, just as the cow made a quick move under Biscuit's neck. Hewey saw her coming and ducked to the left of the charging cow, just as the calf jumped to its own feet and ran.

The tip of the cow's left horn never touched Hewey, but it did hang his shirt, just under the sleeve. The cow never slowed, and Hewey was jerked off his feet as his shirt was ripped almost off his body. He rolled over and sat in the dirt, watching the cow and calf flee through the low mesquites.

"Damn, Biscuit, you'd think they might be at least a little bit grateful." He looked up at the brown horse, which had unconcernedly begun cropping a patch of grama grass. "And why in the hell didn't you keep her off me?"

The next several days presented nothing but more of the same—gathering and counting cattle, punctuated occasionally with the treatment of a wormy cow or calf. Tommy and Enrique talked constantly of the swindle that was apparently being perpetrated by Senor Fat, as they had both taken to calling Fat Gervin.

At the end of the two weeks that it took to count all the cattle, Hewey and most of their horses were tired. Tommy and Enrique seemed no worse for wear, a testament to youth. The cattle count, and Hewey felt fairly confident in its accuracy, was right at four hundred and fifty head. That was about fifty head short of what the count should have been, according to the contract, but even Hewey felt that might be a difficult thing to prove.

What he felt was black and white was that the cattle were not as described. Only about fifty of them could be called Hereford or even crossbreds. Hewey was certain of this. What he was not certain of was what exactly to do about it.

Chapter Nine

Hewey and Spring left the next morning for Upton City, Hewey to ask Fat Gervin what the hell he thought he was doing and Spring to keep her husband out of trouble, although she claimed it was to do a little bit of shopping. Hewey did not believe her, but it really did not matter much what he believed. She was going, and that was that.

They took the buggy since they needed a few supplies and groceries from town. Hewey tied one of Alvin Lawdermilk's geldings behind the buggy, partly because it would do the horse some good, but also because he felt naked without a saddled horse nearby.

A few miles from town they began seeing woolly sheep grazing the pasture on one side of the road. Sheep were not an unusual sight in the area any longer, but this flock was larger than any Hewey had seen in Upton County.

"This is old Vernon Evans' place," Hewey said. "I can't believe that contrary sucker would trade his cattle for a bunch of stinkin' sheep."

They had traveled another half mile or so when they passed a dead dog hanging from the barbwire fence that contained the sheep. The dog, large, brown and of unknown heritage, hung by its hind legs, which were tied to a cedar fence post with a short piece of wire.

Oftentimes ranchers hung dead coyotes on fence posts in this manner. Hewey had seen it many times over the years. Some said it frightened other coyotes, dissuading the predators from entering a pasture. Hewey had never believed that. He figured those doing the hanging just liked to brag to the neighbors that they had killed a coyote. But, in all his travels, Hewey had never seen a dog hanging from a post.

The team of gray geldings were moving at a long trot, and Hewey did not check them as they passed the dog. He and Spring both studied the dog in silence. Fortunately, the wind carried away the foul smell they both knew must surround the decaying carcass.

Finally, Hewey said, "Dern, but you don't see that every day, do you?"

Spring cast a curious look at Hewey, then a similar one back at the dog. She did not know what to say. Three fence posts later they came upon another dog, this one spotted yellow and white but hung from a cedar post just like the first.

"What in the hell is goin' on here?" asked Hewey. He had never been much of a lover of dogs. Spring was not either, although she had a bigger soft spot than her husband. She was becoming offended.

"I don't know, but obviously someone hung them there."

"I figured that," said Hewey. "But what in the hell

for?"

They passed another dog displayed in similar fashion, and then ahead they saw a saddled horse standing near the fence, and just beyond it was a man who appeared to be tying something to a fence post. The outskirts of Upton City were only another half mile farther ahead.

The man finished his vulgar task just as Hewey pulled the grays to a stop. The man's face and hands were browned and lined from many decades of sun and wind. On his head was a battered felt hat that looked almost as old as the man. His shirt and pants showed no newness, either. He gave Hewey a challenging look over the fence.

"Howdy, Mister Evans," said Hewey. "Remember me? Hewey Calloway."

Evans growled, "Hell yes, I remember you. Just didn't recognize you, right off, sittin' in a buggy. You used to be a cowpuncher, seems like."

Hewey smiled. Vernon Evans had never been called nice, nor polite for that matter. "Still am, I suppose. This is my wife, Spring."

"The schoolteacher," said Evans. "From out to the Lawdermilk place."

Spring only nodded. She could have overlooked the gruffness, but there was still the matter of the dead dogs. Both she and Hewey waited, hoping Evans would explain himself. He did not.

"I see you got yourself some sheep," Hewey said.

The Blessing

"You get out of the cattle business?"

Evans turned a slow half-circle, looking over his pasture that contained nothing but sheep grazing the short grass. "You see any cattle?" he demanded finally.

Hewey had spent too much time around old-school cowmen to be bothered by a little grouchiness. "I thought they could be over the hill, or behind a bush."

The grizzled man stared at him, gauging Hewey's sincerity. He had never cared for smart-aleck types. Finally, "Sold my cattle. Sheep make more money, and it don't hurt as bad when they run over you."

Hewey nodded, then looked at the dog with a questioning glance. Evans still took no hints. "You have any problems with coyotes gettin' in these sheep? We been hearin' coyotes nearly every night."

"I'll tell you somethin' about coyotes, and wolves, too. Used to be big lobos here, 'til we killed all them sumbitches out. Everybody gets real nervous when they hear 'em howlin' at night. Thing is, Calloway, it ain't when they're howlin' that you got to worry. The time to worry is when you *don't* hear 'em."

Spring and Hewey exchanged quizzical glances. Evans went on, "Besides, I can handle the coyotes pretty good. It's these goddamned dogs been givin' me fits."

Hewey seized the moment. "Mister Evans, what are you hangin' them on the fence for?"

A smile threatened to cross the man's face, but it

never made it. "All them damn fools in town, they all think they got to have a dog or two or three. Ain't none of them put 'em in a pen or tie 'em up or nothin'. Ever since I got in the sheep business, them damn dogs been comin' out here and killin' my sheep."

Evans paused as he stuffed a large wad of chewing tobacco in his mouth. "I been shootin' ever' dog I see, but damn it, they get new ones faster'n I can kill the old ones. 'Bout a month ago I put an advertisement in the newspaper there in town, said I was goin' to shoot ever dog I catch on my land, and then I was goin' to hang 'em on the fence so everyone could see."

"There's a newspaper in town now?" Hewey asked.

Evans' glare hardened. "Damn it, Calloway! That ain't the point."

Spring nudged Hewey with her elbow. She knew he was intentionally prodding the man.

"Well, sir," said Evans. "Them damn fools didn't listen, seems like. Or hell, maybe they don't read the paper. I still been shootin' dogs out of my sheep, and I been hangin' ever one on the fence, jus' like this son of a bitch here."

Hewey studied the dog. He saw the old man's dilemma. It was tough enough to make a living with livestock without the neighbors' dogs killing stock. Still, this tactic seemed a touch extreme. He said, "I reckon some of those folks got upset with you."

"I don't give a damn what they think. They don't

like it, they can keep their goddamned mutts at home, not out here killin' my sheep."

"Yes, sir. I reckon so." Hewey saw no point arguing with the man.

"That damn sheriff Wheeler come out here the other day, tryin' to tell me I ought not be doin' this. I told him this was my land and I'll damn well do as I please."

Hewey was ready to leave, and he correctly assumed Spring was as well. "Good to see you, Mister Evans, but we best be goin'." Evans was fired up, and Hewey sensed more pontification was forthcoming. He eased the gray geldings into a walk.

"You got any dogs, Calloway?"

"No, sir. None."

The man squinted at him, skeptical. When they were out of earshot, Spring asked Hewey why Vernon Evans was so contrary. "He seems mean, even," she said.

"I guess he's got a right to be thataway. Mister Evans was one of the first white men in this part of the country, maybe even before C.C. Slaughter and old Eli Jessup. All I know is what I been told, but they said Mister Evans had a wife then. She died havin' a baby, there in Mister Evans' house. The baby, a little boy, he lived a day or two, seems like. They're buried not far behind the house."

Spring's eyes glistened, but she had no reply. Hewey stared straight forward as the gray geldings trotted side by side, nearing town.

"He don't ever talk about it. Sure hasn't to me. But years ago, back before there were fences, I was workin' for the Two Cs and was huntin' strays. I rode over onto his place, and I went by the house to tell him what I was doin'. I found him out there at his little cemetery, layin' on the ground, right in between those graves. I just slipped off, quiet as I could, and he never seen me."

Spring did not reply, so Hewey continued. "Somethin' I've thought about since that day. It had to have been ten, maybe fifteen years after his wife and son died that I found Mister Evans out there, layin' on the ground beside them. That's a long time to stay so sad."

Tears streamed down Spring's cheeks then, and she forgave Evans for his demeanor. She still could not forgive the business with the dogs, however. "That's a hurt that won't ever go away, I guess," she said quietly.

Hewey wished then that he had never told her the story. He tried to cheer her mood, something that was becoming increasingly difficult as the years passed. "Did I ever tell you the story about the horse trader sellin' the blind mule?"

Spring thought about that. Hewey had told her so many stories they often ran together. She was quiet, her emotions still not in check. "No, I don't think so."

They had made it into Upton City, and Hewey slowed the team to a walk. "One day this feller bought an old mule from a horse trader. Next day he comes back and tells the horse trader he wants his money back, that the mule's blind. The wise old horse trader tells the man that the mule ain't blind."

Hewey pulled the team to a stop outside one of the two cafes in town, but he stayed in the seat. "This feller tells the horse trader the mule dern sure is blind, that the night before it run into a fence so hard it knocked itself down. It got up and ran across the corral and smashed into the fence over there, then turned and run straight back across and knocked itself down again."

Spring waited, her sorrow turned to amusement, for the moment at least. Hewey had always been good at that, and she loved him for it.

"That ol' horse trader, he looked that feller in the eye and said, 'Mister, that mule ain't blind. He just don't give a damn.'"

A faint smile crossed Spring's face. The story was not that funny, as far as Hewey's stories usually went.

"Mister Evans, he's like that mule," Hewey said. "He just don't give a damn anymore."

Spring was glad Hewey had chosen to eat dinner before going to the bank. She hoped it might improve his mood some. He had been angry when they began the trip to town, but then the strange meeting with Vernon Evans had mixed the anger with a sort of melancholy feeling.

There were three automobiles in town, which did not help Hewey's mood any either. He could remember once seeing two automobiles in Upton City at the same time, so the small community had obviously gone downhill since his last visit.

The small cafe was not busy, since the lunch rush was over, if one had ever begun. Hewey exchanged howdies with a couple of customers. One was a local farmer named Smith, although Hewey could not remember his first name. He knew the man lived north of town, not too far from Walter. He was middle-aged, tall, thin and worn.

The farmer's wife sat next to him at the table. She was a short, plump woman with a sour demeanor. Hewey wondered idly if the food didn't agree with her.

Smith seemed inclined toward conversation. His wife did not. He asked Hewey if they had come from the south, to which Hewey said yes, they had.

"You see all them dogs?" asked the farmer.

The question brought a frown from Spring, almost as cross as the one on Mrs. Smith's face. It was not a topic Spring cared to discuss at the table.

Hewey did not share her compunctions about acceptable dinner topics. "We seen 'em. We even talked to Mister Evans a little. He seems fired up about losin' sheep to the town dogs."

"I got some sheep of my own, and we lost some to a neighbor's dog a year or two ago. So, I can see his plight," said Smith. He laughed a little then. "I tell you what, though. Ol' Mister Evans, he ain't goin' to win any elections amongst the town folk. I guarantee you that."

"Well," Hewey looked at Spring and winked. "I don't reckon he gives a damn."

They both ordered hamburgers and fried potatoes. They had each eaten a couple of hamburgers previously, but they were still a bit of a novelty.

Hewey studied his burger. "You know, this is probably what we ought to do with all them skinny Longhorns Fat stuck us with. Those cows won't make much in the way of steaks, but I bet you they'd be all right ground up like this."

Spring thought he might be onto something there. She had cooked enough Longhorn meat over the years to know it was often short on flavor as well as tenderness. She told Hewey she was going with him to the bank. "I think you'll watch what you say a little better if I'm there, and so might Mister Gervin."

Hewey did not mind and had been expecting it. She was right, halfway at least. *He* would probably choose his words more carefully if Spring was there, although he doubted that son of a bitch Fat Gervin would.

"Suits me," he said, getting up to pay for their meal. "But if things get rough, be ready. If Fat gets me down and sits on me, I'm a goner. Be ready to whack him on the head with a chair or somethin'."

Spring just sighed and shook her head.

Hewey and Fat Gervin had first met a couple decades earlier when they were both cowboys for C.C. Tarpley, or at least when they were both on the payroll. Fat had never been much of a cowboy. He was constantly getting bucked off, and several times he even got lost on the drives, which was a wonder to everyone else, considering the general flatness of Upton County.

The biggest obstruction to Fat's skill as a cowboy had been his lazy demeanor, which was known far and wide to be considerable. If there was a way to shirk the work, Fat found it. He and Hewey had clashed almost instantly back then.

Hewey, as was his nature, had eventually moved on from the Two Cs. Fat, as was his nature, had somehow smooth-talked C.C. Tarpley's daughter into a marriage of convenience, at least for Fat. He found it convenient to work very little, live off his father-in-law and then eventually inherit the man's hard-earned wealth.

The lobby of Tarpley Bank and Trust was dim and cool when they walked inside. Hewey was surprised that Fat had not changed the name to the Gervin Bank and Trust, but he figured perhaps Tarpley's daughter might still hold some sway in the matter.

There was a teller at the first window. She was young, brunette and pretty. Hewey figured if she was also naïve, or perhaps even dumb, then she would be just Fat's style. The teller did not sound dumb, though. She was calmly explaining something to an exasperated, gray-haired and gray-whiskered man in a worn straw hat, overalls and work boots. Hewey did not know exactly what was happening, but the man was upset about some bank policy.

At the next window was another young teller, this one blonde, curvy, and giggling at something Fat Gervin was whispering in her ear. Fat still lived up to his nickname, and he appeared to have bulged even more since the last time Hewey had seen him. He wore an off-white suit with a string tie, odd dress in West Texas, for certain. His black hair had thinned. Fat had grown the sides long and combed the fine hairs over his shiny scalp. Hewey stared at the hairstyle for a few seconds, wondering idly if it had ever fooled anyone.

Fat Gervin had never been an attractive man, not by anyone's standards, yet somehow he had always been possessed of an unaccountable level of confidence when it came to the opposite sex. This confidence often manifested itself into behavior that was overly forward and occasionally bordered on predatory.

Somehow Fat had talked C.C. Tarpley's daughter, Doreen, into marriage, which had mystified everyone, Tarpley most of all. What none of them ever realized was that all the young men in the area had been so frightened of Tarpley that they never made a pass at his daughter. Fat Gervin won her by forfeit. He was the only suitor.

Time and marriage had not tempered Fat's lustful ways. Wise mothers steered their daughters the other direction when he entered a room or walked down the street. However, after he married into money, there were a few females of questionable motives who became somewhat more forgiving of both his looks and personality. Hewey suspected the blonde teller might have been one of these.

He and Spring stopped in front of the blonde teller's window. Fat was practically drooling over her and seemed to be trying to look down her blouse from over her shoulder. The young woman focused her attention on them, but it took Fat a stroke or two longer to pull himself back to reality. A scowl came over his face as recognition struck.

"Hello, Fat," said Hewey cheerfully. Spring nudged him in the ribs. She had asked him more than once not to use the nickname.

The teller's eyes flickered, whether from surprise or amusement Hewey could not tell. Fat Gervin's eyes flickered also, but it was not amusement that caused the light.

"By God, Hewey Calloway, I've told you many times not to call me that. My name is Frank, and you know it. I haven't forgotten who hung that awful nickname on me back in the old days."

The brunette teller at the first window and the

bewhiskered farmer had ceased their argument and were both staring unashamedly at the rapidly escalating disagreement.

Hewey knew everyone was listening, and he liked it. "Oh hell, you was already Fat when I first met you." He paused mischievously. "Both in name, and shape." He demonstrated Fat's round figure with his hands.

"Hewey!" Spring admonished sharply.

Fat's face turned crimson, and small beads of sweat formed on his forehead. He searched for a response, but nothing immediately came to mind. *This is my bank*, he thought to himself. He would not stand for a drifting cowpoke like Hewey Calloway to speak to him that way, and certainly not in front of his employees and customers. That realization struck him. He glanced around and found everyone staring back at him.

The conversation was getting off track right from the start, just as Spring had feared it would. "Mister Gervin, it might be best if we could have this conversation somewhere more, well, private."

Hewey was warming to the moment. "I don't mind who listens. They ought to know what Fat's been doing."

The bewhiskered farmer chimed in. "Hell, I'd like to hear it, myself."

Fat took a deep breath, realizing the soundness of Spring's suggestion. "Yes, perhaps we should step into my office, although I do not see what business I could possibly have with the likes of a cowpuncher like Hewey Calloway."

"Breach of contract, maybe even stolen cattle, Fat," said Hewey. "That's the business we need to discuss."

"I have no idea what you are talking about," said Fat as he hurriedly walked through a door to the side of the tellers' windows and shuffled toward his office.

Spring followed him, but Hewey paused and looked at the blonde teller. "Don't you believe everything ol' Fat tells you. Him and the truth ain't ever been close friends."

The blonde smiled knowingly, and Hewey followed Spring and Fat Gervin into a large office in the corner of the bank. It was walled off from the rest of the building, although there was a glass window looking into the lobby. Fat shut the wooden door behind them. The brunette teller and the bewhiskered farmer watched closely, but Hewey saw the blonde teller hurry out the front door of the bank.

Fat's face was still red, and the beads of sweat on his forehead had grown into droplets. Hewey guessed correctly that the cream-colored suit was becoming damp. "Dammit, Calloway, I ought to have you arrested for coming into my bank and making a spectacle, telling lies in front of my employees and customers."

"You best hold off with the talk about havin' people arrested. You get the law involved, *you* might be the one gettin' arrested, Fat." Hewey enjoyed using the nickname, because he could see the man's irritation each time he said it.

"What the hell are you talking about?" Fat demanded loudly.

Spring cut in, her voice calm and even. "Hewey, Mister Gervin, both of you, please, let's keep this civil."

Hewey nodded and smiled at his wife in acknowledgement, then winked at Fat. "You're right. I'll be civil, long as *Fat* is."

Fat steamed for a few seconds, then asked, "Why are you here, Calloway? I have no time for your nonsense."

"I'm here, Fat, because you sold part of C.C.'s ranch, the old Simmons place. I'm sure you remember. It's ours now." Hewey chose his words carefully. He could not say Fat had sold it to him, and he did not want to say it had been given to him. He was still somewhat uncomfortable with that idea, and he certainly did not want Fat Gervin knowing the details.

Fat stared, incredulous and momentarily silenced, then stuttered, "You? I don't believe that. How? The buyer went through an attorney, and I never knew. How did *you* buy it?"

Hewey ignored the questions. He had only told those details to Walter and Eve and had dodged a few questions from others. There was no way he was giving the specifics to Fat Gervin. "The contract stated that there would be 500 head of cattle, all Hereford or Hereford crosses. There ain't but a handful of that kind of cattle out there, and you know it. You either lied from the beginning or pulled some kind of switch afterward."

Fat had regained some of his composure, and Hewey could almost see the devilish wheels turning inside his perspiring head. An evil smile formed on his face, and finally Fat replied. "I looked through those cattle myself. In my opinion, they were all fullblood Herefords or crosses. I reckon I can spot a good cow better than you ever could, Calloway. Best I can tell, their bloodlines are strictly a matter of opinion. I cannot see how you could prove anything."

It was Hewey's turn to get angry. "Fat, every cowman and half the farmers in Texas can tell the difference between a Longhorn and a Hereford, and you know it."

The devilish smile grew on Fat's wide face. "I'm not so sure about that, Calloway. But for argument's sake, say they could tell the difference. Could they prove it? Legally, that is? I don't believe so."

Fat Gervin had been known to pull some shady business deals over the years, but the threat of having a falling out with his father-in-law had kept him somewhat reined in. Now that C.C. Tarpley was gone, it seemed that Fat was running unchecked. Hewey's temper flared. "You fat son of a bitch! You'll make this right or I'll give you the whippin' you've deserved for twenty years."

Spring noticed Fat Gervin's right hand slip under his desk, and she wondered if he might have a gun under there. It made sense, in a bank. She placed a hand on Hewey's leg. "Enough, Hewey," she said.

Jumping to his feet, Hewey answered, "It ain't enough. Not nearly enough. Fat, you've always had the conscience of a coyote and about as much class as a red-headed buzzard."

Suddenly there was a loud knock on the office door, and it immediately opened. Sheriff Wes Wheeler stepped into the room. "Sit down, Hewey," he said sternly. The blonde teller stood outside the door, a look of concern on her face. Wheeler glanced back at her and said politely, "Thank you. I believe you were right."

"Sheriff, I'm sure glad you're here," said Fat. "Calloway came in here with wild accusations and then threatened me with physical violence. I want him arrested."

The sheriff held up a calming hand. "Now hold on, Mister Gervin. I'm not certain that will be necessary."

Wes Wheeler had gray hair that matched his mustache. He was tall, lean and could get harsh on the rare occasion when a serious criminal came to Upton City. He and Hewey had been friends of a sort for fifteen or twenty years. The friendship was strong enough that Wheeler might help Hewey if he could do it easily and legally, but Wheeler would not bend the law for him. As for Fat Gervin, Wheeler did not like him any more than most of the other decent folks in the county did. However, the owner of the biggest ranch in the county, and the only bank in town, had a considerable amount of political pull, and Wheeler liked his job.

Wheeler said, "Mrs. Calloway, I get the feeling you might have the coolest head in the room just now. Why don't you tell me what's going on here?"

Fat moved as if he were about to speak, but Wheeler held up a hand to silence him. "Go ahead, Mrs. Calloway."

It took several minutes for Spring to go through the story, and twice Fat Gervin attempted to interrupt but was stopped by the sheriff each time. Hewey, surprising everyone, sat in calm silence.

When Spring was done, Wheeler asked Fat if he would like to add anything, which he did. "I can't have bums like Calloway barging in my bank and causing a scene. I want him arrested, sheriff."

"Arrest Fat for cattle theft, while you're at it," added Hewey.

Fat's face was turning red again. "I didn't steal anything, Calloway."

"Gentlemen, please," said Wheeler, although he did not feel like either was being overly gentlemanly. "Frank, I can't arrest Hewey for anything. It seems you invited him into your office, so he wasn't even trespassin'. Hewey, you know there's no way I can arrest Frank for cattle theft over this."

"How about breach of contract?" asked Hewey.

"That would be a civil matter. I expect you would need an attorney to file a civil claim. That is not my jurisdiction."

Hewey grinned at Fat. "Well, I might have to do that."

"I am not frightened of that. You have no case, Calloway." But everyone in the room saw Fat Gervin's skin turn from red to white as he contemplated a lawsuit.

Hewey seized the advantage. "I never filed a lawsuit in my life, Fat, but that don't mean I can't learn how. I bet the same lawyers that helped buy the ranch would be tickled to do this for me."

Wes Wheeler stepped forward, between the men. "That's enough, fellers. Hewey, Mrs. Calloway, I think it's time for us to go. Frank, would you just stay in here for a few minutes until we're gone?"

No one spoke, and no one offered to shake hands as they left. The bewhiskered farmer loitered in the lobby, too curious to leave. As they stepped out of the bank and into the hot sun, Wheeler told Hewey to stay away from Fat Gervin.

"I heard about him pulling a shotgun on you that time a few years ago. I don't need any shootings around here, especially not over this. You hear me, Hewey?"

"Hell, Wes, I ain't gonna shoot anybody. I'd like

to give him the whippin' he deserves, is all."

Wheeler told Hewey that also would not be tolerated, despite the logic. "You just steer clear of Fat for a while, all right?" Wheeler paused, then asked. "Hewey, I got to ask. Just how in the hell did you end up with a ranch anyhow?"

Fat Gervin lumbered from the main house at the Two Cs headquarters, across the hard-packed dirt to the worn board-and-strip bunkhouse that stood near the barn and corrals. Fat had lived in that bunkhouse twenty years earlier, but it held no sentiment in his mind.

Doreen Gervin, Fat's wife, still lived in the house where she had grown up, along with their children. Fat stayed in town most of the time. He was no more a devoted father than he was a devoted husband. He claimed the arrangement was for convenience since he spent his days at the bank rather than at the ranch. Doreen knew better, but for many years their relationship had run more smoothly the less they saw of each other.

It had surprised Doreen when her husband had driven up to the house that afternoon in his black automobile. She had not expected him until Friday evening or possibly even Saturday morning. He had business with the cowboys, he had told her brusquely.

The Two Cs cowboys saw Fat coming and slowly

gathered on the porch. They were mostly a ragtag lot. The good hands had slowly left the ranch after C.C.'s passing, unable to get along with his son-in-law. C.C. Tarpley had been as tough as he was tight, but his men respected him. Fat was just as tight, but that was as far as the similarities went. Those Fat hired to replace the departing cowpunchers were questionable of both skill and moral fiber.

The wagon boss was a man named Burgin Stamp. Whispers said Stamp had spent time in the penitentiary at Huntsville, but no one had summoned the nerve to ask the man. He was a decent cowman, although he had a tendency toward cruelness, particularly with horses.

Stamp did the duties of a normal ranch foreman, but Fat had retained that title for himself. He did occasionally give an order at the ranch, but it had been fifteen years since he had straddled a horse.

The men stood in a rough semicircle around Fat, who had relaxed his weight on a wooden chair on the bunkhouse porch. They eyed him warily, one snake always recognizing another.

Sweat ran from under Fat's short-brimmed straw hat. He patted his face with a blue handkerchief. "Boys, I need to talk to y'all about something."

He always talked to the cowboys as if he were one of them, but even the dimmest among them saw straight through it.

"A few weeks ago y'all moved some cattle around, tryin' to sort them old Longhorns from the better cows.

Me and Burgin, we thought that was the best thing to do for the ranch."

Burgin Stamp studied Fat with unblinking eyes. There had been no such decision, not that he was part of anyway.

"Well, I sold that Simmons place, and now the new owner is throwing a fit about them Longhorns, saying I done him wrong. You men know me. You know I wouldn't ever intentionally do wrong to another man."

Several of the men exchanged glances, but none spoke.

"I don't know for sure what's going to happen, but I need a favor from you boys. If someone was to come around here asking questions, I need y'all to just forget about us sorting those cattle. I ain't doing nothing wrong, mind you. I'm just trying to avoid a disagreement, you see."

The men did see. They saw right through it.

"But to show my appreciation for your," Fat paused, looking for the right word. "For your cooperation. I'm going to give ever' one of you a five-dollar bonus this month."

There were only six men on the crew, but the cost still rankled Fat. Five dollars would not buy many men, but this crew was easily swayed and he knew it. All except for one man, the lone holdout of the old Tarpley crew.

Durwood Todd sat on the edge of the porch, not

looking at Fat. He had worked for C.C. Tarpley for several decades. Todd was a short man, gone slightly soft in the middle. He was one of the old-time cowhands who did what he was told and expected little in return. He had the skill to have taken on more responsibility over the years, but he lacked the desire.

Fat had been planning to fire Todd, because the man's apparent loyalty to C.C. Tarpley rankled him. Todd, in his opinion, was too old for the job anyway. It never occurred to Fat that Todd could do more at sixty than Fat ever did at twenty.

The aging cowpuncher felt Fat's gaze, but he chose not to acknowledge it. He felt nothing but disdain for Fat Gervin. He only stayed on at the ranch because he knew finding another cowboy job at his age would be difficult, if not completely impossible. So, he stayed there on the new Two Cs, choking down more disgust with each passing day.

Finally, Fat said, "Do you understand what I'm saying, old timer?"

Todd simply stared at the ground beneath his feet, packed hard from years of boots tromping in and out of the bunkhouse.

The other hands were watching, and it caused Fat's face to redden. "I'm talking to you, Todd. Do you understand what I'm telling you?"

Durwood Todd turned his head and looked up at Fat, who was twenty years younger and a hundred pounds heavier. Fat could not hold the gaze, and he looked away. "Yes, sir, Mister Gervin." His tone held none of the respect the words implied. "I understand exactly what you're talking about."

"That's good," said Fat, back in control. "You best remember it, that damned Hewey Calloway comes around here. All of you."

Todd's eyes flashed, then narrowed at the mention of Hewey Calloway. He said nothing, just slowly turned and resumed staring at the hard-packed ground between his run-down boots.

Chapter Ten

Hanley Baker gave up and set *The Wyoming Tribune* on the table next to his coffee cup. He sat musing in silence for several minutes. His wife, Samantha, occasionally looked over the top of her book but said nothing. She felt certain she knew what her husband was thinking, and she was fairly certain what he would decide, even if he still did not.

They lived in a small home on the outskirts of Cheyenne, for the moment at least. They had chosen to stay there after they were married, since it was home to Samantha. Baker did not exactly have a home. He had a cabin and some land in Colorado, but Texas still felt like home to him.

Baker had left the Texas Rangers years before. The Rangers at that time had been a place for young men, and he had the misfortune to become an older man. He had chosen to leave, a decision he often regretted.

After Baker left the Rangers, he cowboyed some and even had a couple foolhardy adventures with Hewey Calloway. Samantha worked in the sheriff's office in Cheyenne. After they were married, Baker had begun assisting there when the sheriff was short-handed. The arrangement worked well for him. He worked enough to satisfy his conscience and fished enough to ward off his natural tendency toward grouchiness, which in turn satisfied Samantha.

Since the shocking gift from the Hendersons, the couple had often discussed moving elsewhere. Cheyenne was a nice town, but both agreed that the winters affected them more each year. Baker missed Texas, and Samantha was open minded.

Baker finally looked up from his thoughts. "What would you say about taking a train ride down to Texas? We could make sure Hewey is staying out of trouble. We might even look around some, see if there's someplace that suits you, someplace you might like to live."

Samantha feigned surprise, although she had been making a mental list of the things she would need to do before heading to Texas, then simply said, "When are we leaving?"

They left the next morning on the train, riding a passenger car headed south. They had the time, and lately they had acquired the means, so they made a leisurely trip of it, stopping overnight several times along the way.

Baker had ridden across most of the countryside they traversed at one time or another over the years, but Samantha had never been south of Fort Collins, Colorado. Denver was too large to suit either of them, but Samantha was enthralled with the portion of the trip south of Denver and through the northeastern tip of New Mexico.

She knew how to get what she wanted from her husband, and she had begun to decide that Trinidad, Colorado, or the vicinity, might be what she wanted. It was beautiful country. She began running her finger up and down his thigh. "Hanley, honey, we might not need to move all the way down to Texas. We could buy a little ranch right around here somewhere."

Baker knew what she was doing but was powerless to fight it. She still held some sort of power over him. It had begun the day he met her years earlier, but somehow it had not waned.

He made no move to stop her suggestive moves but said, "Stop that, woman. I've told you before, this ain't a fair way to fight."

She moved closer to him, rubbing against him slightly. "Who's fighting, darling?"

Baker leaned his head back and closed his eyes. "Oh, hell," he groaned.

Samantha laughed, a deep, husky laugh that weakened his resolve even further.

They crossed the Texas Panhandle, which still intrigued Baker even after all the hard miles he had ridden across the open and often waterless plain. Samantha, a mountain girl at heart, was less impressed with the scenery.

They reached San Angelo late in the day and checked into the Hotel Concho, which was near the train station and alongside the Concho River. Baker figured to stay the night and buy some horses in the morning. They had brought their saddles on the train. Baker had ridden the same saddle for over thirty years and was partial to it.

He did not know where Hewey's new ranch was located, other than it was in Upton County. However, he knew Hewey had family there, and he had first met Hewey years before at Alvin Lawdermilk's ranch. Hewey would not be hard to find.

It took Hewey Calloway three days to cover the hundred miles between his ranch and San Angelo. The advice Morgan Jenkins had given him about setting up a line of credit had been on his mind, and it had become more pressing as their meager cash supply continued to dwindle. Hewey had little experience with banks, and none of it had been pleasant.

It was a chore he would have preferred to skip, but he saw no alternative. The banks were closed by the time he rode into San Angelo. He had noticed over the years that bankers seemed to want their borrowers to work their fingers to the bone, yet the bankers themselves started late, quit early, and often closed the bank altogether.

It had been several years since Hewey had been to San Angelo, and the town had grown considerably. He found a saloon on Concho Avenue that seemed to cater to cowboys. It was still early in the evening, so the drinking crowd was thin. There were ten or twelve younger cowboy types standing along the bar and sitting at the scattered tables.

The middle-aged bartender slid a beer to Hewey with a silent but polite nod. Hewey scanned the crowd and found he did not recognize a soul in the place. There had been a time, one that to Hewey did not seem so long ago, when he would have known half the cowboys in any saloon in West Texas and part of New Mexico.

A touch of sadness crossed his mind when he looked over the cowboys again, more slowly this time, and realized he was the oldest among them. It hurt even more when he realized he was *twice* as old as most of them.

Where the hell has time gone? he wondered to himself, not for the first time. He still needed another hand at the ranch. However, after a study of the young men in the saloon, he decided they were probably more mouth than anything else. He would likely be better off short a man than with one of these. He finished his beer and asked for another, this one in a bottle.

He laid money on the bar, and then stood to leave when the bartender handed him the bottle. "The town police don't allow people to drink on the street no more," the bartender advised.

Although he was a little older and a little tamer, the old Hewey Calloway was still in there. "What kind of town is this? Folks can't even drink a beer outside?"

And he walked out the door, beer bottle in hand. The town police could go to hell over that one.

Hewey woke early in his bedroll, which he had laid out under some trees down by the Concho River. It was not too far from where Walter had his leg broken in a fight so many years earlier, a fight caused by Hewey. That one still troubled his conscience at times, because he knew Walter's leg still troubled him at times.

Pincushion was staked along the riverbank, with one of Alvin Lawdermilk's broncs nearby, which he had brought along as a pack horse to carry a few supplies not easily found in Upton County.

He found a cafe that opened early. He ordered fried eggs, bacon, hashbrowns and biscuits. There were a couple older men at a nearby table. They were dressed too nicely to be cowboys, but both had hats hung on the chairs next to them. Hewey exchanged good mornings with them, then asked if they could recommend a bank in town that might loan money to a poor rancher.

One of the men was thin with a tan, creased face. He paused his fork in midair, egg yolk dripping, and asked what sort of loan Hewey had in mind.

"I don't rightly know, not exactly," Hewey said. "I never borrowed money from a bank in my whole life. I got a ranch all of a sudden, and I need some money to buy some supplies and pay some cowboys, for a little while at least."

The other man at the table had been studying him, and he pointed at Hewey with a half-eaten piece of toast. "Ain't you Hewey Calloway?"

It was not the first time Hewey had been recognized by someone he did not know, so he was not too surprised. He had on occasion made a spectacle of himself and been remembered for it later. "Yes, sir. I reckon so."

The man smiled. "Never met you myself, but I've known who you are for a lot of years. Heard a lot of stories," the man said, smiling. "You still a hellraiser?"

Hewey grinned faintly, remembering. "No sir, not so much, I reckon. I'm gettin' old, got me a wife. Guess I've settled down some."

"That might not be such a bad thing, from some of the stories I heard about you." The man chuckled, then looked at his companion, who was still eating. "Hewey here, him and this other feller are the ones roped that automobile a few years ago. Tore the hell out of it, if I remember correctly."

Hewey held up a hand and shook his head. "Nah. Just tore it up a little bit."

The second man, the talkative one, continued, "Things were more fun back in them days. Before everyone got so damn serious." He paused, remembering, then continued. "So, you got you a ranch somewheres, and a wife? Got any young'uns?"

"No sir. I don't," said Hewey.

"Hell, it ain't too late," said the second man. "You ought to think about it. Ain't nothin' better."

Hewey did not answer. He didn't know what to say.

"Where's your place?" asked the man.

"South part of Upton County," Hewey answered.

"Why don't you do your banking closer to home?"

"I ain't on real good terms with the banker in Upton City. Me and him got some bad blood."

The first man studied him in silence, then said, "I have heard some about that man. Frank Gervin, isn't it? From what I hear, he is a man of questionable moral principles."

Hewey smiled and nodded his head slightly. "That's puttin' it lightly, mister."

The thin man looked at him a moment more, then said, "Mister Calloway, I am the manager at First National, two blocks south of here. We open in an hour or so. My name is Thomas Quill. I grew up on a small ranch south of here a few miles. My older brother still runs it. I know the cattle business. Come see me."

Hewey brightened. "Yes sir."

The talkative one advised, "If you really need a banker, Calloway, you best do it. Tom's about the nicest banker around here. He'll suck your blood 'til you're plumb dry, but at least he's friendly while he does it."

The Blessing

A couple hours later Hewey emerged from the First National Bank of San Angelo in a daze. He had a checkbook in his pocket, the first checkbook he'd ever had, and Thomas Quill and the bank had a lien on his ranch. He got a better feeling about Quill than he did from most bankers, but even so, he felt he had better be cautious with his new line of credit. It might be better to just give the checkbook to Spring, he told himself.

He pulled the cinch a couple holes tighter, stepped on Pincushion and headed down the street. He was looking for somewhere to buy Spring a couple new books and a newspaper. Ahead he saw a crowd gathered, and curious, he rode that way. Just beyond the commercial district was a set of stout, well-used wooden corrals, the people congregated near them.

A short, slightly round man with a greasy beard and shifty eyes stood on the bed of a wagon parked outside the corrals, speaking loudly to the crowd.

"All you got to do is saddle that old paint and ride him 'til he quits, or to the count of thirty," said the man, pointing at a small and pretty sorrel tobiano paint horse that stood idly at the far side of the corral.

After a short pause, the man went on. "Any man can put up whatever bet he wants, so long as it's twenty dollars or more. If he can get the paint rode, I'll pay back five times the bet. FIVE TIMES THE MONEY!"

Hewey whistled quietly. *Five times the money*, he thought to himself. This was the sort of challenge that had always called his name. He pulled his bad leg from the stirrup and flexed it, feeling the stiffness and soreness in the knee. He thought about Spring. He thought about the new ranch and the lien he had just given to Thomas Quill. He thought about all that responsibility, and the sad fact that he was getting older. He frowned, shook his head almost imperceptibly, then relaxed back into the saddle and just watched.

"I'll give any taker twenty minutes to get him rode!" the man on the wagon said in not quite a shout. "If you can't do it in twenty minutes, well, you probably ain't gonna get it done noway."

The man looked over the crowd. There were some lively conversations taking place. Some of the younger men were joking and pushing each other, trying to get their buddies to step up even though they themselves did not have the nerve. Still, there were no takers.

"I'll be honest with you folks," said the man on the wagon. "It's been a while since Ol' Paint was ridden, been a little while since anyone even got a saddle on him, to tell you the truth. It's been done, but it takes some doin'. It takes a good hand to get it done. Ain't there any *real* cowboys in San Angelo?"

Hewey noticed a young man at the edge of the crowd digging through his pockets, counting what money he found. He was very young, maybe still a teenager, Hewey thought. His skin was brown, and Hewey pegged him as a Mexican. He was handsome, dressed like a cowpuncher, with faded Levi's and a well-worn, long-sleeved shirt. He wore a black felt hat and pale shotgun chaps. A pair of chihuahua spurs hung from worn boots. The thing that set him apart, though, was the black hair that fell nearly halfway down his back.

The young man appeared to have counted all his money, because he stared at it a moment, frowned at it, and then shoved the money back in a front pocket of his pants. Hewey waited for him to move toward the front, but he stood still.

Still mounted on Pincushion, Hewey rode along the rear of the crowd to the long-haired cowboy. He was not even sure why he did it. "You gonna enter up?"

The young man looked up at him in surprise. His eyes were almost black, and they seemed to glow. "The man said you had to bet twenty dollars. I don't have enough."

Hewey had halfway expected Spanish but heard only a slight accent. "You think you can ride that old paint?" he asked.

The young man shrugged indifferently. "Sure. Why not?"

The casual confidence struck a note in Hewey, and he dug in his own pocket. He counted everything. Sixty-seven dollars. He was supposed to bring a few things back to Spring. *Oh well*, he thought. He pulled off the two one-dollar bills and offered the rest. "I'll back you. We'll divvy it up afterward."

The young man looked at him curiously, flashed a broad smile, then moved through the crowd to the man in the wagon. Hewey watched them talking. The cowboy handed over the money, which the man counted.

"Ladies and gentlemen, we have a taker! This boy has bet eighty dollars, which I must say is a confident wager indeed!"

The young man walked back through the onlookers and beyond to where a horse was tied to a fence by a bridle rein. The horse was short and broad, a nice-looking black gelding with a Rafter G branded on its left hip. Hewey wondered briefly about the brand but could not place it.

Moving quickly and smoothly, the young cowboy unsaddled his black horse. He left the saddle blanket on the horse's back, taking only his saddle with a rope tied to the horn.

Back at the corral, the man in the wagon handed him a braided hackamore with horsehair reins. The young man inspected the hackamore, opened the corral gate and walked into the pen.

Holding up a metal watch, the man in the wagon said loudly, "Twenty minutes starts now!" Several of the spectators looked at their own watches. The crowd had grown, and Hewey saw his new banker, Thomas Quill, watching from the other side.

"You back that boy?" someone asked Hewey. He had been looking in the pen and had not seen anyone walk up to him. He looked down to see a very old, very small black man leaning on a cane, looking not at him but instead into the corral. The man looked like many of the grizzled cowpunchers he had known over the years. Too worn to do it anymore but not so old that they didn't miss it.

"Yes, sir. I did."

"I expect," the man said, "you made a good bet."

Hewey looked down at the old-timer, who was still staring into the corral. "You know him?"

The man still did not look up at Hewey. "No, sir. But there's somethin' about that boy, can't really say what it is. I jus' get the feelin' he knows his way around a horse, or somethin'."

Hewey did not know what that meant, the last part. It did not bother him so much then, but he wondered about it later.

Inside the corral, the young man had swung his saddle over the top rail of the fence near the gate, then took his rope loose from the saddle. He also took a shorter tie rope that had been hanging from the swells of his saddle. This he simply draped over his shoulder.

"Be a damned sight easier if they was a snubbin' post," commented the old man beside Hewey.

Hewey did not look down at the man, but said, "What do you reckon he's plannin'?"

"Don't rightly know, but I believe we're about to find out," the old man said.

The cowboy built a loop in his rope and took a few

steps toward the paint, which shifted its weight and cocked an ear, eyeing him. The young man took another step toward the horse, which changed its demeanor in an instant and ran straight at him, teeth bared.

Hewey knew from experience that it took far more nerve to face a charging horse than a cow or even an angry bull. Horses were smarter, and the few that would actually make a run at a man usually meant business.

With his rope held casually at his side, the young man waited until the paint was almost upon him, then he quickly stepped to the side. The paint went past, and he brought up his rope, took one quick swing and roped the horse by both front legs. He pulled the tail of the rope behind him and leaned back on it. The rope pulled tight on the paint's front legs, and they were jerked from underneath it.

The horse's momentum was too great. Its head hit first, and then almost instantly it turned a full somersault across the hard, dusty ground of the corral.

This was not the first time the paint horse had been handled by someone with skill, and it was not without skill of its own. It jumped to its feet quickly, as if expecting the man with the rope to attempt to hold it down. Instead, the young man pitched slack into his rope and allowed the paint to walk out of the loop. The move surprised Hewey and the rest of the onlookers, and it seemed to surprise the horse as well.

The Blessing

The cowboy built another loop and stepped toward the paint, forcing it to move along the fence and to the right. The horse hit a lope, and the young man brought up his rope and took an overhand swing. Sensing what was coming, the paint slid to a stop and reversed direction.

Watching, Hewey knew it was much more difficult to forefoot a horse traveling right to left than the other direction. It was even impossible for many.

Without stopping his rope, the young man changed the arc of his swing. He took two swings down by his side, then threw an underhanded loop that snaked across the corral and directly into the path of the horse, again catching it by both front legs.

"That boy savvies the mangana," said the old man with the cane.

The young man pulled the rope behind him again, leaning back on it. The paint went down with an audible thud. Shaken, this time the horse paused for a second after hitting the ground, and this time the cowboy did not.

Holding the rope tight so that the paint's forelegs stayed pulled up to its body, the long-haired cowboy quickly closed the distance and knelt on the horse's neck. He dropped the loop of his tie rope over the right front foot, then pulled the tail over the horse's neck and around it. He tied it back to itself with a slipknot, short enough that the horse could not extend its leg.

The horse was fighting and thrashing, attempting

to reach back and bite the man on its neck, who for a moment seemed concerned as he looked at the hackamore hanging from the saddlehorn of his own saddle, which was on the fence fifteen feet away.

An onlooker outside the corral moved as if to pick up the hackamore, but the man in the wagon shouted at him. "No outside help!"

Suddenly the young man jumped and ran for the fence, grabbed the hackamore and headed back. The paint was still thrashing, trying to get to its feet, but one of them was tied to its neck, hindering its movements. Still, the paint was making progress when the cowboy made it back and again knelt on its neck.

Despite the thrashing and biting, the cowboy soon had the hackamore tied on the horse's head. The morning air was hot and humid with no breeze, and both man and beast were sweating.

"Still gon' be hard to get a saddle on that paint sumbitch without a snubbin' post," the old man told Hewey, who agreed. The horse might have a leg tied up, but once on its feet, it would still be able to move around enough to make things difficult.

The young man tied one of the hackamore reins to the right foreleg, the one that was tied up to the horse's neck, and then he stepped back and watched.

The paint began to thrash again, trying to get to its feet. It was a difficult maneuver, since one leg was tied up and its head was tied to that same leg, albeit loosely. Still, it only took a few seconds for it to stand. The horse took a couple of breaths, then it tried to run. Hewey was not certain if it was trying to get away or get to the cowboy. Whatever its motivation, the paint stumbled and almost fell, though not quite.

The young man calmly walked to his saddle, took it off the fence and headed back. The horse's head was tied to the right, so despite its desire to bite the cowboy, it could not reach him when he approached on the left. The young man unbuckled his cinches from the keeper, and when he set the saddle on the paint's back, both cinches were already hanging down.

Cautiously, the cowboy reached under the paint's belly and grabbed the front cinch. The horse tried to cow kick him but, athletic and motivated as it was, could not do so with its front leg tied to its neck. The cowboy soon had both cinches tight. He stepped around to the right side of the horse and carefully untied the paint horse's head, but he left the leg tied up.

"TEN MINUTES REMAINING!" shouted the man in the wagon.

The young man seemed indifferent to the time constraint. He calmly walked back around to the left side of the horse, which was still fighting as best it could. The cowboy crossed the horsehair reins over the paint's neck.

Beside Hewey, the old man said, "Now comes the hard part, maybe."

Hewey was not sure. "I get the feelin' this might not be too tough for that boy."

"Yessir, you and me both," said the old man.

In the corral, the young man dodged the paint's teeth and stepped into the saddle. The horse quivered but stood mostly still, knowing its leg was still tied up. The cowboy leaned down and pulled the tail of the rope, releasing the slip knot that held it.

The paint horse was an old hand, and it knew its rider was leaning down and toward the right to untie the rope. The instant the horse was free it dropped its head between its front legs and leaped to the left in an attempt to jump out from underneath the rider. It hit and began bucking seriously, kicking higher with each jump.

Hewey watched in admiration. In his day he had been an excellent bronc rider, far better than average though occasionally thwarted by his own recklessness. Nonetheless, he knew immediately that he had never been in the same category as this long-haired boy.

The paint began bawling with each jump, and the young man even smiled a little. He began reaching down at the bottom of each jump, raking his chihuahua spurs along the horse's shoulders as it came up again. He was always half a jump ahead of the horse, as if he knew what would happen next. It was all so *casual*, Hewey thought.

"Son of a bitch," said the old man with the cane.

"You ain't kiddin'," answered Hewey.

Several members of the crowd had been counting out loud, obviously hopeful the rider would hit the thirty-second mark that would win him the bet with the man in the wagon.

The paint tried every trick it knew, and it had learned more than a few tricks in the several years it had traveled the country with the man in the wagon. The young man met each one with ease and what might have even been relish. Later, in the saloons and cafes around town, onlookers would talk of how the young cowboy seemed to be enjoying himself atop that bad paint horse.

The crowd's volume increased at the count of thirty, and then cheers erupted. The young man gave it another couple seconds for good measure, then kicked loose his stirrups as the horse came upward. He flew from the paint's back and landed on his feet, stumbled as he looked back at the horse, then trotted to the safety of the fence.

"I never seen anything like that," said the old man beside Hewey. "He made it look so damn *easy*."

Hewey grinned in admiration of a kid he did not even know. "He did, but you and me both know there wasn't nothin' easy about that."

"You got that right," said the old man.

Hewey slowly rode through the throng of onlookers to the gate, which a bearded man in bib overalls opened and let him through. Hewey rode over to the man in the wagon and said, "You didn't say nothin' about gettin' the saddle off afterward. I'm gonna help that boy."

The man glared at Hewey, obviously upset with the outcome, but he nodded slightly. Hewey trotted Pincushion around to the paint, which allowed him to reach down and pick up a hackamore rein. He dallied it short to his saddlchorn, watching the paint closely. He had seen it try to bite the young man earlier.

The boy walked up and watchfully unbuckled his cinches, then pulled off the saddle. "Thanks, mister," he said with a bright smile.

Once the young man was safely near the fence, Hewey reached over and untied the throat latch, then pulled off the hackamore. The paint horse slowly eased away, acting like a gentle saddle horse.

Hewey watched as the long-haired cowboy walked to the wagon. The owner was now next to the wagon rather than in it, and he seemed none too pleased. He very rarely had to pay, since the paint horse was so tough, and he had never been forced to pay on such a large wager. Hewey kept an eye on the man in case he tried to renege on the bet.

The man had tried that once several years earlier in East Texas, back before he had found this paint horse. He had learned then that local crowds could quickly turn violent when one of their own is being cheated by an outsider. So, reluctant though he was, he counted out four hundred dollars to the smiling young man.

It took several minutes of back slapping and hand shaking by grinning locals before the long-haired cowboy could make his way to where Hewey waited in the shade of a big mesquite tree, holding his horse by a bridle rein.

Hewey was grinning as the young man walked up. "That was a heck of show you put on, you know that?"

The cowboy smiled slightly and shrugged, as if it were no big deal. Hewey stuck out his hand. "I'm Hewey Calloway."

Taking his hand, the young man responded, "Boone Baca."

Something flashed far back in Hewey's brain, as if that name were somehow distantly familiar, but he could not place it. "Where did you learn how to handle a horse like that?"

"I don't know," said Baca. "Just always sort of came natural to me. Ever since I was a little kid."

Baca pulled out a folded stack of bills and counted out three-hundred and twenty-five dollars, Hewey's share. He was evidently as good with figures as he was with horses, Hewey realized.

Hewey had an idea. "Say, you ain't lookin' for a job, are you? I got a little place out west of here and could sure use another hand."

Shaking his head, Baca said, "Thank you, but I'm headin' northwest, up to the Llano Estacado."

"That's some big, lonely country. I been through there many a time and worked up there some," said Hewey. "What's up there for you?"

Baca looked off, sort of wistful. "I don't know, not

really. Just never been up there, never seen it, but I sort of feel drawn there. Can't say why."

Hewey thought he understood. He had traveled many miles for no more reason than that. "Well, you look me up if you ever get to Upton County. My place is on the south end of the county."

"Sure thing, Mister Calloway. Maybe I'll stop by on my way home from the Llano, but I can't say when that'll be."

"Where's home?" Hewey asked.

"You probably never heard of it," said Baca. "Little ejido south of Ojinaga."

When Hewey turned to walk away, he was surprised to see his friend Hanley Baker standing nearby, smiling at him. He had only seen Baker smile a handful of times, so that shocked him almost as much as seeing Baker in Texas. He was supposed to be in Wyoming. "Hanley, what in the hell are you doing in San Angelo, Texas?"

Baker walked toward him, a slight hitch in his step, then stuck out a hand. "Well, I hadn't checked on you in a while and figured you'd had enough time to get yourself in trouble. Thought I better come see for myself."

"Hell," Hewey said, shaking Baker's hand firmly. "I been stayin' so far from trouble it doesn't even know where to find me."

"Yeah, I bet," Baker said, knowing better. He looked Hewey up and down, noting the new wrinkles and some gray hairs peeking through. "Damn, Hewey. You got old."

Unoffended, Hewey said, "Well, you been old."

"Ain't that the truth?"

"You didn't bring your wife with you?"

"Samantha's at the hotel. I was goin' to find some horses to buy. We rode the train from Cheyenne to here, then we were plannin' to ease down to Upton County and find your new place. I heard you got yourself a ranch."

Hewey eyed him. "You heard, did you? The way I understood it, you had a hand in it."

"Would you have took the money if they offered it?"

"No," Hewey conceded. "And I'm surprised you did. You're more stubborn than I ever been."

"I don't know about that. But the difference is, I'm smarter."

"If you're so smart, why didn't you just ride the train to Rankin? The railroad runs a few miles south of my place. Been a whole lot closer than San Angelo."

Baker thought for a second. "I never even heard of Rankin, and I been all through that country with the Rangers. Last time I was down that way, wasn't any railroad either."

"You got to keep up with progress, Baker, or you'll get left behind. That's what I always say."

Baker looked at Hewey's horse. "Why didn't you take the train?"

Hewey shrugged, indifferent. "Never thought of it 'til I was halfway here."

They walked to the hotel so Hewey could say hello to Samantha. The two had met only once several years earlier during a hectic evening in Cheyenne. Samantha was older than Hewey but younger than Baker. Hewey had been as smitten with her as Baker had been. She had aged slightly since then, Hewey noticed, although not necessarily in a bad way.

Samantha hugged him tightly. He could feel her body through her thin dress, and it embarrassed him. She saw it and was amused. "Hewey! I didn't expect to see you here. We planned to ride to your place and see you in a few days."

"Well, I had to come to town, do some bankin'."

Samantha laughed, the same husky laugh Hewey remembered. "Banking? My, how things have changed." She looked at Baker. "Did you find us some horses?"

"No, not yet." He pointed at Hewey. "I went lookin' for horses and wound up with a stray dog instead."

"Shoot, I was hoping old age had cheered you up. That was too much to ask for, I guess." Baker was known for his occasional grouchiness, which for the most part bounced off Hewey.

Samantha was enjoying the conversation. "You

ought to try living with him."

"Ma'am, I traveled with him enough to know," said Hewey.

"It's like living with a sore-footed bear, and that's on the good days," Samantha said.

"I had a little grullo horse one time. He come out of Mexico. Mean little sucker. Couldn't nobody get along with him. Funny thing is, his name was Hanley when I bought him. I didn't even know Mexicans used that name."

Baker cut in before Hewey could go any further with his story. "If you two are just going to gang up and pick on me the whole time, maybe y'all ought to just ride along together and I'll follow behind somewhere out of earshot."

"That's the best plan I heard all day," Hewey said.

They went down to the wagon yard. Baker needed three horses—two saddle horses and another to carry a pack saddle. Between Samantha and him they had far more belongings than they could carry on their saddle horses, most of it hers.

"I should've brought my little pack mule," Baker said. "See if you and him can get along any better than you used to."

Baker had a little gray mule that had taken an instant dislike to Hewey years earlier in Colorado, and it had demonstrated its feelings by quickly kicking Hewey. The relationship had never recovered.

"I figured that little bastard would've died of old

age by now," Hewey said.

"Nah, he's too mean to die."

It took nearly an hour of negotiating and bickering before Baker and a practiced horse trader made a deal. Both stomped around pretending to be mad at each other, but in the end, they settled on a fair price.

"You sure these horses are old man gentle?" Hewey asked the horse trader.

Baker grumbled something indecipherable under his breath. He had their saddles, but buying a pack saddle from the trader took another ten minutes of arguing. Hewey helped Baker saddle the new mounts. He noticed Samantha would ride a regular cowboy saddle, not a sidesaddle.

"Spring used to ride a sidesaddle, but she won't anymore," he said, cinching up the bay horse Baker had bought for Samantha. "She wears pants and boots most of the time now, too. A couple of days a week she goes out with us and helps. She's a pretty good hand."

Baker said jokingly, "Next thing you know, these women'll be wantin' to vote." He paused and looked at Hewey. "But then again, I'm sure they'd do a better job of it than you."

"Hell, I don't even vote. Never have," Hewey said. "I don't ever know when they're takin' a vote 'til it's over."

"My point exactly," said Baker.

Chapter Eleven

It took Hewey, Samantha and Baker four days to ride back to southern Upton County, a day longer than it had taken Hewey to make the same trip alone. Although Baker was a former Texas Ranger and was still tough as nails, he was no longer a youngster. Samantha, for her part, would not be hurried if it did not suit her, and it did not suit her. Hewey was anxious to get back, but good manners kept him civil. He did not hurry them.

It was dry in San Angelo, which was not unusual, but the farther west they traveled, the drier it became. Baker had spent most of his life in Texas, but he had lived in a wetter climate for the last several years.

"I nearly forgot how dry it is out here," he remarked.

"It needs to rain, that's for sure," Hewey agreed. "I guess it has to one of these days."

The wind was blowing out of the west, almost into their faces. Baker said, "The oldtimers used to say that it won't rain until the wind quits blowin' out of the west, and the west wind won't quit blowin' until it rains."

Hewey had heard that one many times. There was some truth to it. After a short silence, Hewey asked Baker if he had seen much of Bob Wilson. They had traveled with Wilson years earlier in Colorado and into

Wyoming. Wilson had been falsely accused of bank robbery, an ordeal that had ended with him wounded and another man dead.

The only good to come of the deal, other than some good stories for Hewey to tell, was that Wilson had met and later married Baker's niece, Daisy.

Baker smiled slightly at the question. "Oh, yeah. We usually go see them about once a month. They got two kids now. A boy and a little baby girl. Did you know that?"

"I just knew about the boy. They send a letter ever' now and then, but we hadn't heard about the little girl."

"Well, she ain't very old. Just a few months, I guess. They named her Martha, after Mrs. Thomas."

"How're they?" Hewey asked.

"Oh, they're doing pretty good. Gettin' older, just like the rest of us. They love Bobby and Daisy's kids like they were their own grandkids."

A few miles later he told Baker all about the issue of the cattle not matching the description in the contract. Baker rode along in silence, his forehead wrinkled as he thought about it. "I don't know. You sure you want to make a fight out of it? Why not be happy with what you got and let it go?"

"If it was anybody else, I might could let it go. Sure, there's the money. The cows they left are worth about half of what was supposed to be there, maybe less than that. But there's more to it. For twenty-five years Fat Gervin has been cheatin' people, and some of them was me and Walter. He tried to steal Walter's farm eight or ten years ago and damned near got it done. My leg hurts ever' day, and I guess it always will. That's on account of Fat sellin' them outlaw plugs to Morgan Jenkins, and that ol' stud damn near killin' me. So, I can't just let it go. Not with him. It's not just the money. It's the principle."

Baker understood that. He would have been the same way. Samantha said nothing, but Baker figured she understood, as well. He had yet to see her turn down an argument with anyone. He asked, "Did you talk to the lawyer in Alpine, the one who helped with the deal?"

Hewey shook his head. "I thought about it. Spring thinks I ought to. But hell, I never much liked lawyers and don't want to mess with one on this, not if I can help it."

Baker was riding alongside Hewey, Samantha listening from just ahead of them. They held their horses to a slow trot, both men leading their pack horses. Throughout their friendship, Baker had often tried to advise Hewey. The guidance typically fell on unconcerned ears. "Hewey, whether you like it or not, you're a ranch owner now. You're a businessman. There may be times when you're goin' to have to talk to a lawyer or do some other kind of distasteful thing."

Samantha laughed lightly when Baker said it would be distasteful to speak with an attorney, but neither Baker nor Hewey knew why she was laughing.

Baker had not meant to say anything funny.

"Reckon I ought to get Spring to write him a letter?"

Baker shook his head. "Dammit, Hewey. Surely there's a telephone in Upton City, ain't there?"

"I don't know," Hewey admitted. "I ain't ever needed one."

"Here's what I think," Baker said. "You talk to the lawyer, see what he says. But it sounds like this Fat Gervin might be the type to take advantage when he can but will cave in if the pressure gets heavy. Is that about right?"

"Yeah, the fight generally leaves ol' Fat if somebody mashes on him."

"I doubt I could scare him much, since I ain't a Ranger anymore. I got no pull. But I have an old friend that I served with. I think he's a captain now, but I'm not real sure. He was out in West Texas and probably still is. He likes it out here. His name's Clarence Rogers. You heard of him?"

Hewey thought about it. "No, don't reckon so. I never done nothin' so bad the Rangers got after me."

From ahead, Samantha said, "Not yet, anyway. The way you two are conspiring, I feel like this could go downhill pretty quickly."

Hewey and Baker looked at each other, and Baker shrugged. He went on. "I don't remember just where Clarence come from, but he grew up hard and poor and it made him tough. He was a Ranger back when they was still chasin' Indians. He's killed a few men, and it never seemed to bother him much. He ain't very big, but he's as tough as they come. He's even a little mean sometimes."

"Maybe he'll just shoot Fat. That'd save the world a lot of trouble."

"Nah, he's still honest, mostly," Baker said. "But somethin' happened with his folks and a bank. It was a long time ago, and I don't know the details. But I do know he's got a grudge against bankers in general, and 'specially them that bully poor folks."

"Poor folks," Hewey agreed. "That's me."

"Sugar," Samantha said from the front and without turning her head toward them. "You ain't poor anymore. You might still think you are, but the rest of the world doesn't see it that way. Believe me."

Hewey said, "Heck, I just had to borrow money, and that was to live on."

"Doesn't matter, Hewey. You and Hanley are now men of means, even if you do still act like regular old common folk."

Baker spoke up. "Don't argue with her. She's gettin' bored up there and lookin' for a debate. You'll lose, I promise you."

Samantha smiled, but they could not see it. Hewey thought about arguing but changed his mind. He asked Baker, "You think your pal Rogers can help?"

"I don't know, not for sure. But I bet he'd think it's fun to put the squeeze on this Fat Gervin. I think you better call the lawyer, and I'll call Clarence. We'll get it worked out, one way or the other."

It was late afternoon when the three of them made it to the H bar C. They found Spring taking down a few dry clothes from the clothesline behind the rock house. She was glad to see Hewey, and she was happy to have some company, in particular some female company. She'd had little female conversation lately, and she missed it.

Baker shook hands with Spring. "Pleased to meet you. I know you must be a woman of infinite patience, being married to Hewey."

Spring laughed, but Samantha still apologized for her husband. "Don't mind him. Hanley's got a smart mouth. It's the smartest thing about him, in fact."

Spring took Samantha inside to get her settled in the spare bedroom. She had not expected company, and she had never met Hanley or Samantha, but she still welcomed them into her home.

Unloading the two packhorses, Hewey told Baker he would catch a couple fresh horses and show him around the ranch before dark.

"You'll have to keep it short," said Baker, feeling his tired and sore body protest the mistreatment he had given it the last several days. "I ain't as young as I used to be."

"I didn't know you was ever young," Hewey

replied.

They left an hour later, both riding fresh horses. They promised to be back in time for supper. Samantha had plans to use the bathtub, which still did not have a fence around it. Samantha did not seem concerned with the lack of privacy, which Hewey found very intriguing. He kept those thoughts to himself.

They all left for Upton City the next morning. Spring knew there was a telephone company in town, which was news to Hewey. The plan was for him to call the lawyer in Alpine who had been involved in the purchase of the ranch, and for Hanley Baker to call his Ranger friend Clarence Rogers.

Spring wanted to go to town for a change of scenery, but she also thought it might be necessary to ward off any trouble should there be an encounter with Fat Gervin. Samantha went along cheerfully.

Tommy and Enrique saddled a couple of young horses, both of them excited since they had not been to town in several weeks. Hewey knew they had been itching to go to town, so he gave them the day off work.

"You boys be back tonight," Hewey sternly told them before they parted in town. He remembered his own behavior at that age, and it worried him. He warned, "And don't do nothin' too foolish." He could almost see his words roll right off them, not even beginning to sink in, and he gave up.

The only telephone in Upton City was located in the telegraph office. A middle-aged man ran the telegraph, and a plump, gray-haired woman served as the telephone operator. The building only had one small room, so the telephone users had no privacy whatsoever.

Hewey politely gave the lady the name of the lawyer, Howard Stephens, in Alpine.

"That's long distance," she said sweetly. "I'll have to charge you."

"That's fine, ma'am," Hewey said.

"It'll be a little while." She pointed at a couple of wooden chairs against the wall near the door.

Hewey felt uncomfortable in the small room. "We'll be on the porch."

Both men were restless by the time the operator opened the door and summoned Hewey. It had been well over an hour, and Hewey had become unimpressed with telephone technology.

The phone was made of wood and metal, with two shiny silver bells at the top of the box. Below those was a black metal tube that protruded from the wooden base. Hewey quickly ascertained he was supposed to speak into it. Another tube, this one attached to the base by a slender wire, he held to his ear. It was all very strange and unfamiliar to him.

Stephens' voice was tinny and distant, and Hewey felt he needed to speak loudly to be heard. Both the telegraph and the telephone operators looked elsewhere, although Hewey knew they were listening. He felt self-conscious, a feeling almost foreign to him.

The Blessing

"Mister Stephens," Hewey almost shouted. "This is Hewey Calloway. You helped us with the ranch contract. The one in Upton County."

Hanley Baker had come inside to listen. He sat in one of the wooden chairs, smiling at his friend's discomfort as he heard Hewey's side of the phone call.

Hewey was silent, frowning as he concentrated. "Yes, that's me," he said gruffly.

He listened for a few more seconds, then gave the lawyer an account of the situation regarding the cattle. Baker gathered that the lawyer was not a cattleman when Hewey was forced to explain the difference in the breeds and the disparity in the value of them.

After another pause, Hewey said, "Well hell yes, I'm sure. That's why I'm callin' you. What can we do about it?"

Lines crossed Hewey's forehead as he listened in silence for a full minute. "That much?" he said finally. After a pause, he said, "Okay, send it. I'll send you a check. All, right, all right. Thank you."

Hewey hung up the phone and looked around the room. Both operators had their heads down, appearing busy, but Hewey had noticed that neither had accomplished much during the call. The gossip would reach every corner of Upton City by that evening. Hewey decided he did not much care.

Baker demanded, "Well, what did he say?"

Looking at the man and woman, Hewey motioned him outside, then said quietly, "He said the first thing is for him to write a letter to Fat, threatening to sue unless he delivers the correct cattle or pays the difference. Said he doesn't know if it'll work, but maybe. And he wants me to send him a check for fifteen dollars. That seems pretty damn high to me."

"Most of them lawyers believe a license to practice law is the same thing as a license to steal. They'll rob you blind, and they don't even need a gun to do it."

Hewey grunted dejectedly, then waved a hand at the door in a silent invitation to Baker. It took another hour, and in the end, Baker was only able to leave a detailed message for Clarence Rogers, who fortunately was still stationed in Midland.

"That's the problem with these damn telephones," Hewey said. "He ain't around one when you need to talk to him, and now you're fixin' to leave and go twenty miles from this one. What in the hell good are they?"

"You just talked on one, didn't you?"

Hewey said, "Yeah, but I know what I'm doin'."

They walked outside, where they found Spring and Samantha headed their way. There had been more than enough time for them to shop at every store in Upton City. There were not many. Baker asked, "Y'all ready to head back?"

Samantha and Spring both shrugged. Hewey said, "Yeah, we better get out of town pretty soon, or Spring'll end up at Dutch Schneider's saloon again.

The Blessing

She got fallin' down drunk the last time we came to town. Be glad you didn't see it. It was plumb embarassin', I tell you."

Spring rolled her eyes but smiled. "Shut up, Hewey."

Tommy Calloway and Enrique Rodriguez had very little idea what to do with their time in town. Tommy had grown up near Upton City, so he was familiar with the town, although in a boyish sense. He had been there very little since reaching adulthood. Enrique had rarely visited any town and never this one.

They wandered around town for a while, but little held their interest for long. They ate dinner at a cafe, but that only killed an hour. Hewey had paid them, so their pockets were full. They had heard all the stories growing up, so they knew cowboys in town were supposed to raise hell. But they were not sure how to go about it.

They came after a time to the doors of Schneider's Saloon, an establishment Tommy knew only by reputation, although he had known the owner since he was a boy. Dutch Schneider was a friend of his father and uncle and had even visited their house on occasion. He had attended Hewey's and Spring's wedding.

Looking up from his newspaper, Schneider eyed the two young men critically as they entered. He stared first at Tommy, then his gaze shifted to and lingered on

Enrique, who began to wonder if the old proprietor might have issues serving Mexicans. Enrique had felt little of that racial bias, although it was mostly because he had hardly been in any town since coming to Texas. Still, he knew the feeling was strong in some.

Finally, in his strong German accent, Dutch Schneider said politely, "You're Walter Calloway's son. Tommy, I believe. Is that right?"

"Yes, sir, that's right." Tommy wondered how much fun he could possibly have in a saloon owned by a friend of his parents. What if Mister Schneider told his mother?

"And you," Schneider turned his head toward Enrique, then looked him up and down slowly. Enrique fidgeted, thinking about turning and fleeing the saloon. The saloonkeeper said slowly, "How old are you, my young friend? You do not seem old enough to be in here."

Enrique looked at Tommy in confusion. What difference did it make how old he was? He had only ever been in one drinking establishment. That had been a cantina in the little town of Potrero del Llano, in Chihuahua. It was small and dingy and had no name that Enrique ever knew. The owner was a lazy fat man named Gonzalvo who held no compunctions about serving minors.

Schneider, who was just as much an immigrant as Enrique, was amused by the boy's discomfort. He fully expected him to lie about his age. Enrique considered it, but he was not given to telling lies. His father had spoken to him many times about the worth of a man's reputation. Also, he was not altogether certain these crazy gringos might not throw him in jail for lying.

The English language escaped him in his nervousness. "Diecisiete," he said truthfully.

Schneider spoke two languages, but neither of them was Spanish. He frowned. Tommy, proud of his own growing understanding of Spanish, said, "He's seventeen, Mister Schneider."

The saloonkeeper made a clucking sound with his tongue and shook his head sadly. "I'm afraid that is not old enough."

"But Mister Schneider, Enrique has a man's job and does a man's share. We both work for my Uncle Hewey."

Schneider's face broke into a smile at the mention of Hewey Calloway. "I had heard my old friend Hewey is back. I would very much like to see him. He is a good man, your uncle."

"Yes, sir. I don't reckon he would mind if you sold Enrique something to drink," Tommy said.

This was not the first time a boy had attempted to sway the saloonkeeper, and he saw through it. "Young Tommy, I will tell you something. It is not so much that I have a problem with serving your friend here. But there are some in this town who condemn me for serving liquor to grown men. It would only fuel their fires to see a couple of young boys in here. It would not serve me well in the community, and especially not in the church."

Hardly a Sunday passed that Dutch Schneider did not attend the morning service, and after all the years, there were still those who questioned the motives of a foreign saloonkeeper worshipping amongst the Baptists.

"I tell you what I will do," said Schneider. "I will bend the rules, just this once. I will serve you each one beer, but one beer only. No whiskey."

"But I'm old enough to order whatever I want," Tommy protested.

"Yes, but I know your mother. She is not a woman I would have angry with me."

Tommy had no argument for that one. "Yes, sir."

They sat at a table near the front, looking out a window. There was little to see. Neither admitted it, but both found the beer slightly unpleasant to the taste. It was lukewarm and bitter. They wondered to themselves what the fuss was all about, but still they both pretended to enjoy it.

Soon their attention was drawn to the other side of the street. A pretty brunette walked down the wooden sidewalk opposite them, headed their way. Their beers forgotten, Tommy and Enrique stared. It was the first pretty girl either of them had seen in quite some time.

Schneider saw their attention shift, and he walked to the door to look outside. He smiled as he saw what had drawn their eyes, remembering his own youth from long ago.

The brunette entered a small grocery store almost opposite the saloon. Tommy stood suddenly. "I'm goin' to talk to her."

Enrique's accent had morphed into a strange mixture of Spanish and West Texas, at least when he spoke English. No one had noticed. "What are you goin' to say?"

Tommy had not thought of that. He had little experience talking to the opposite sex. His nervousness grew. "I guess I don't know."

"My young friend," said Schneider. "If I may, just start by telling her your name and asking hers. And try not to act so nervous. The rest will come."

Enrique beamed. This was more excitement than he had expected. "I'll come with you."

Schneider placed a hand on Enrique's shoulder. "I think your friend will be better off alone. You stay with me."

Enrique narrowed his eyes at the man. First he didn't want him there, and then he wouldn't let him leave. *Crazy gringos*, he thought.

Tommy brushed off his clothes, wishing he had washed them before coming to town. Then he wished for a moment that he had washed *himself*. He strode across the empty dirt street and onto the wooden sidewalk. He paused briefly outside the grocery store, willing himself on, then opened the door and stepped inside.

A little silver bell tinkled above the door, causing the only two occupants of the small store to turn and look at him. A bald storekeeper sitting behind a counter and holding a flyswatter looked at him with bored eyes, then turned back to the book he had been reading.

The pretty brunette stood between two wooden shelves sparsely stocked with canned goods. In one hand she held a small cotton sack with the word RICE printed across it in big letters, and in the other hand was a single potato.

The girl, Tommy judged, was about his age or perhaps a touch older. She was not very tall, and slim. Her brown hair hung halfway down her back. She gave Tommy a quizzical look with what he thought were the prettiest brown eyes he had ever seen.

Dutch Schneider's advice long forgotten, Tommy stood frozen. The storekeeper looked up again, still saw nothing of interest, and went back to his reading. The girl cocked her head slightly, her expression one of puzzlement. Tommy stared back at her, his own expression blank. Finally, she asked, "Is everything alright?"

Tommy blinked hard, his stupor broken, then somehow found his tongue. "Yes, ma'am. My name's Tommy. I seen you come in here, and well, you're the prettiest girl I ever seen and I just wanted to say hello."

The girl was surprised. She smiled shyly, although she liked the attention. "You're pretty forward, ain't you?"

Tommy was not sure what that meant, whether it was compliment or rebuke. "I don't know about that, ma'am. What's your name?"

She looked back at the shelf, studying the canned vegetables. She had successfully fended off the constant advances of Fat Gervin for nearly a year and was in good practice. The difference here was that she was enjoying these advances.

"Leta," she said without looking at him. "Leta Montgomery."

Tommy's shyness was washing away by the second, replaced by unearned youthful confidence. He asked, "You're not from around here, are you?"

"How would you know?" she teased. "I've never seen you around here before."

In unnecessary detail, he told her how he had grown up nearby but had been working on the Circle W south of Alpine, and that he was now helping his uncle on a ranch out south of town. The words flowed out of him.

Done with her shopping, Leta made her way to the counter. Tommy followed. He casually leaned on the counter as she paid for her few groceries. The storekeeper looked at him with annoyance. In the man's opinion, ranch owners were occasionally good customers. Young cowpunchers like this one had never brought him anything but annoyance. When they came to town, it was not for groceries.

"May I help you, young man?" The clerk's tone

was anything but helpful.

Tommy was oblivious to the man's sarcasm. He answered without shifting his gaze from the girl. "No, sir. I'm doin' just fine."

Leta smiled coyly. "You certainly think you are, don't you?"

"Five minutes ago I was trying to choke down a lukewarm beer and now I'm havin' a conversation with the prettiest girl in West Texas. So yes ma'am, I reckon I'm doin' just fine."

The clerk snorted aloud. He had never resorted to such foolishness when he had courted his wife, Edna. That Edna's width had deterred all other suitors never occurred to him.

Leta gathered her two purchases, thanked the clerk and headed for the door. Tommy stepped around her and opened it, causing the little bell to tinkle again.

"Thank you," she said as she stepped outside. She continued to walk, but her stride was slow, hopeful. She need not have worried. Tommy closed the door and quickly caught up with her.

He offered to carry her groceries, but she declined. He asked, "Is that what you're plannin' to eat tonight?"

"Yes, it is." Mister Gervin did not pay well at the bank, so she was frugal when it came to meals. She kept these details to herself.

Tommy walked a couple of strides before speaking. "Well, that stuff ought to keep 'til tomorrow. Why don't you let me buy your supper at one of the cafes?"

Leta looked at him out of the corner of her eye. She had very little experience as far as actual courting went, but she had certainly never met anyone so bold. She looked back up the street in the direction of the two cafes.

"I don't even know your name," she said.

"I told you, it's Tommy."

"What's your last name? I can't go to supper with someone if I don't even know his last name."

"Oh, sorry. It's Calloway. My name is Tommy Calloway."

She paused, wondering. "Any relation to a man named Hewey Calloway?"

Tommy grinned. Everyone loved Uncle Hewey. "Why sure. That's my uncle. I work for him even."

Leta looked at him sharply, which confused Tommy. He gave her a puzzled look in return. "I work at Tarpley Bank and Trust," she said. "For Mister Gervin."

"Oh hell," Tommy said involuntarily, then caught himself. "Sorry for that."

She shrugged. Mild bad language did not bother her the way it did her mother. "Mister Gervin does not speak well of your uncle. The sheriff was even called when they had a confrontation in the bank."

"That don't have nothin' to do with us," argued Tommy. "Besides, you don't mean to tell me you work for Fat Gervin and still trust him all that much, do you?"

Leta thought about that one for a few seconds. In point of fact, she did not trust Frank Gervin any farther than she could throw him, and she knew she could not begin to even lift him. Still, she needed the job, so she said nothing.

Tommy felt the momentum shift back in his favor. "Come on. Let's go down to the cafe. We'll talk about somethin' else. Their problems don't have to be our problems."

Leta was dubious. She felt certain Mister Gervin would make it her problem if he saw her associating with a family he seemed to hate with such passion. Still, she relented. "Okay, I'll go."

Tommy was so ecstatic that his feet barely touched the ground as they walked down the wooden sidewalk. He saw Enrique looking curiously out the window of the saloon, and he grinned.

Chapter Twelve

The following week held more manual labor than any on the H bar C crew preferred. Tommy and Enrique could work horseback from sunup to sundown and never complain, but when Hewey told them they had to shore up the corrals at headquarters and then build a chute, the griping began.

C.C. Tarpley had never been one to spend money unnecessarily, and in his opinion, corrals were unnecessary. His cowboys could hold a herd of cattle as well as a corral could, and cowboys were cheaper. Evidently the previous owner, Bill Simmons, had held similar feelings. There was one set of corrals on the entire ranch, and it was those at headquarters.

Hewey, for his part, did not have much use for corrals, either. He had learned the cowboy trade in the open range days when there were not even pasture fences. Now, though, he needed to burn his brand on several hundred grown cows. There was no practical way to do it other than with a chute. They would rope and drag the calves, but Hewey knew they could not rope all the cows, certainly not with his small crew.

The lumberyard in Rankin began delivering cedar posts and rough pine planks. Hanley Baker helped some, but he held the same cowboy dislike of working on foot as the others. Since he was not on the payroll and thus not obligated, he often sat in the shade and offered unsolicited advice.

Hewey liked the work as little as anyone, but he was surprised at the pride he began to feel, looking over their progress. If Tommy and Enrique felt pride in their work, they hid it well. Their complaints were always in good humor, but they were endless.

"Next thing you know," Tommy told Enrique while Hewey was only a few feet away, "Uncle Hewey is goin' to start plowin' up the pastures so he can plant cotton."

"At least I'll have a couple farmers on the payroll already," Hewey snapped back.

Samantha Baker often sat with Hanley and watched, entertained by the banter. She had been around plenty of cowboys in Wyoming, but these Texans were a different breed.

One morning Enrique paused while digging a post hole, the sweat running down his face. "You know, Mister Hooey. I think maybeso you should get some Mexicans to do this. I hear those people are hard workers, and they are good at building things."

"You do realize you're a Mexican, don't you?" asked Hewey.

"That's what I always thought, but now I'm not so sure," said Enrique. "I think I must be a gringo."

Hewey paused. "Why's that?"

Enrique could not help but grin. "Because I'm not

so good at hard work."

Tommy held up to the work, although his after-hours activities had begun to limit his sleep. Every few days he headed for Upton City as soon as the day's work was done, and he came dragging back late in the night. Leta always sent Tommy on his way in the evening, never allowing him to stay late. She knew how ruthless small-town gossip could be. It seemed to Hewey like his nephew went to a lot of trouble just to see a girl for only a couple hours.

Usually, on the mornings following Tommy's late-night trips to town, he was slow to breakfast. One morning he was there early, anxious to tell the news he had heard. Spring was still cooking when he burst into their house.

"Uncle Hewey," he said excitedly. "I got some news for you!"

Hewey stared at him expectantly. He thought Tommy would continue unprompted, but he did not. Finally, Hewey asked, "Well, what is it?"

"Leta said two days ago Fat Gervin got a letter in the mail. She don't know what it said, but after he read it Fat was stompin' around, talkin' to himself and cussin' you."

A broad smile slowly spread across Hewey's face. Hanley and Samantha had come in from the spare bedroom and had heard the news.

Hanley, a cup of coffee in hand, said, "That has to be from your lawyer."

"I reckon so. I sure didn't write any letters myself," Hewey said.

"What did it say?" asked Tommy. He and Enrique did not know the details.

Hewey took a drink of coffee. "All I know is it was goin' to say Fat done a breach of contract by switchin' the cattle, and he could make it right or get sued."

Tommy was still excited. "What do you reckon Fat is goin' to do?"

From the stove, Spring admonished, "You better quit callin' him Fat. Call him Mister Gervin."

"Yes ma'am." Not one person in the room expected him to do it, though.

"I don't know what ol' Fat is goin' to do," Hewey said. "He'll fight it someway. He's too much of a shyster to just give up."

"Hewey, these boys will continue to call him Fat as long as they hear it from you," Spring said, without turning from the stove.

Winking at Tommy, Hewey said, "Do what she says. Respect your elders. Even the sons of bitches."

They were taking turns digging a post hole in the hard ground inside the corral when Tommy looked up and saw a rider trotting up the dirt road that led to the headquarters. "Somebody's coming."

All were eager for a break, so they stopped to look. The man slowly trotted his horse down the road, then slowed to a walk as he drew closer. From his chair in the shade, Hanley Baker said, "That's a lawman. I can tell by the way he's actin'."

Hewey recognized the rider then. "That's just Wes Wheeler. He's the sheriff."

Wheeler drew up twenty feet from the working men. Spring and Samantha had seen him coming and were walking out, curious about the rare visitor.

"Howdy, Wes," Hewey said cheerfully. "You come to do some real work? We got an extra shovel."

His face serious, Wheeler shook his head. "I'm afraid I'm here on official business, Hewey. I hate like hell to have to do this, but I've come to arrest you."

Hewey grinned uncertainly. Wheeler seemed serious, but he could not figure why. "Arrest me? For what?"

"Attempted murder. Somebody shot Frank Gervin, and he says it was you."

Spring gasped audibly. Hewey was confused. Everyone was quiet, looking at the sheriff or exchanging glances with each other. Finally, Hewey said, "I guess Fat's still alive, if he's talkin' to you."

Wes Wheeler only nodded. It was obvious he did not enjoy the situation.

Baker spoke from his chair in the shade. "When was this?"

"Last night, right after dark. I heard the shot myself, but by the time I got to Mister Gervin's house there wasn't nobody there but him."

"Hell, Wes, I was here last night. I ain't been to town in days. Everyone you see here will tell you that."

Wheeler looked around at them all, seeing confirmation in their faces. It only made things worse for him. "Hewey, you got to see my predicament here. I can't for the life of me believe you'd shoot anybody."

Baker and Hewey glanced at each other. Hewey had in fact shot someone years before in Colorado, but it had been not only justifiable but had been completely necessary at that moment. Only a handful of relatives and close friends knew about that event. It was one of the few stories Hewey did not like to tell.

Wheeler went on. "That said, once the doctor got Mister Gervin sort of patched up and he got to where he could talk some, he told me you had burst into his house there in town and shot him with a pistol."

"He's lyin', Wes. You have my word I didn't shoot Fat. Been a lot of times I'd have liked to do it, but it wasn't me."

Wheeler admonished, "Sayin' things like that ain't goin' to help you."

"How bad is Mister Gervin hurt?" Spring asked.

"He'll live," said the sheriff. "The bullet hit him sort of low on the side. The doc said it didn't hit nothin' vital."

"I expect it'd take a buffalo gun to punch through all that lard," said Hewey.

Wheeler gave him a hard look. "This is more serious than you think, Hewey. I hate to do it, but I have to arrest you. I'm not jokin'.'"

Another small gasp came from Spring, and she went to Hewey's side. She placed an arm around him protectively. "Hewey was here last night, sheriff. He had nothing to do with this, I promise you. I think you know that, too."

Wheeler rubbed his temples as if his head hurt. "Y'all got to understand. The man who owns the bank and one of the biggest ranches in the county is tellin' me Hewey shot him. I don't much believe him, but I got to do my duty. We'll sort this out, but for now I got to take Hewey in."

Hewey's shoulders slumped for a second, then he pulled himself out of it, for Spring's benefit. He took both her hands in his. "Don't fret too much about this. There ain't no way this'll stick. You know that."

He gave Tommy and Enrique some instructions on what they should do in the coming days.

"How long's this goin' to take, Wes?"

Wheeler shook his head. "I can't say, Hewey. You know there ain't no full-time judge in the county. I'll have to send for the circuit judge. It's been so long since anything like this has come up, I honestly don't know what's about to happen."

"Can't I get bailed out or somethin'?"

"Maybe," Wheeler said. "But that's not up to me. Still got to wait on a judge."

Hewey looked at Baker, who was still sitting in the shade. He had a small smile on his face, like he was in a good mood. Baker said, "I know I ain't been much help lately, but this sounds like somethin' where I might can be of some use."

The sheriff eyed Baker suspiciously. "Who are you, mister?"

Baker thought about standing and offering a handshake, but the sheriff did not give off a welcoming feeling. "My name's Hanley Baker. I was a Texas Ranger down in the Hill Country for twenty-five years."

"Not anymore?" asked Wheeler.

"No, sir. Retired."

"In that case, I don't want you meddling in this. It's complicated enough as it is."

Baker did not like the tone. "I reckon as long as I don't break any laws, you ain't got much say in what I do."

Hewey cut in. He preferred to keep Wheeler on his side as much as possible. "Wes, give me a minute to change into some clean clothes. These are a little rank."

Wheeler nodded, still eyeing Baker. Hewey asked Tommy to saddle Pincushion for him. The dun horse was in the corral and would be convenient to catch.

Little was said while Hewey went to the house. No one knew what to say. Tommy returned, leading the dun horse, just as Hewey emerged from the house. Spring and Hewey hugged, and he tried to raise her spirits by joking that at least he didn't have to dig the remaining post holes. The joke fell flat. He looked at

Baker, who nodded in silent understanding. Hewey grabbed the saddlehorn and stepped onto the dun. Wes Wheeler had never dismounted.

"I'll see y'all in a day or two," Hewey said with feigned cheerfulness as they rode away toward town.

Enrique was confused and looked as if he might cry. Tears ran freely down Spring's cheeks as Samantha wrapped her arms around her. "You Texans," Samantha said. "You sure like to keep everything lively, don't you?" They all stood and stared, uncertain what to do, until Hewey was out of sight.

Sheriff Wes Wheeler and Hewey rode north toward Upton City at an easy trot, side by side down the dusty road. They said little to each other. Hewey felt a faint sense of betrayal by his old friend and was in no mood for trivial conversation. Wheeler, for his part, was nagged by guilt over what he was doing. He saw no way around it, considering the circumstances, but he took no joy in it.

After several miles of quiet, Hewey finally said, "Wes, you know I didn't do this. You ain't really goin' to let Fat railroad me all the way to the penitentiary, are you?"

Wheeler looked as if something pained him inside. "I had to do this today. You got to understand that. It's my job. When someone gets shot and then tells me who done it, I have to listen. It don't matter who they are, on either side of the situation."

It seemed to Hewey that Wheeler had more to say, so he did not answer. The sheriff slowly gathered his thoughts as their horses trotted north. "That being said, you're a long way from a trial and even further from the penitentiary. I promise you I'm goin' to look into this, and same as I said before, it don't matter who's in it. I'll be fair. I promise you that."

It took Hewey a while to think that over. "That's all I can ask. Thank you, Wes."

The sheriff did not answer. He didn't feel he had done anything to be thanked for, not yet.

A couple of miles farther along, they met three riders followed closely by an ancient chuckwagon pulled by two sorry-looking gray mules. One of the wagon's wheels was warped enough that it wobbled with every revolution, leaving behind a serpentine track in the dust. The tarp covering the wagon was ripped in multiple places, offering little protection in the unlikely event that rain should fall. Hewey wondered idly if the wagon would make it out of the county.

The riders pulled up, as did the wagon when it caught up with them. Wes Wheeler and Hewey drew rein, curious. The small caravan did not fit into any normal category of traveler.

The four were dressed as cowboys, and unprosperous ones at that. None of them appeared to be much past his teens. They were all dusty and travel-worn with several days' growth of soft whiskers on their faces. All but one seemed amiable, a couple cheerful even.

One of the youths stepped his bay horse close to Hewey and offered his hand. "Howdy," he said respectfully. "I'm Eldred Sheets. Over there is my brother and a couple of our amigos."

Hewey shook hands, taking an instant liking to the boy's jovial manner. "I'm Hewey Calloway, and this here is Wes Wheeler. He's the sheriff."

The boys all offered their howdies, although from the sullen one it seemed forced. Eldred Sheets looked at Hewey. "I know who you are, Mister Calloway. We're from way up in the Panhandle, but I been hearin' stories about you since I was a little kid."

Hewey thought Sheets might *still* be a kid, but he did not say so. Wheeler acted anxious to be moving along, but Hewey felt no need to hurry, not where he was headed.

Sheets continued. "There was an old man helped us some back home. He said he worked with you out in New Mexico a long time ago. He was always talkin' about you, tellin' wild stories."

"What's his name?"

"Arthur Dorn, but he got killed two, maybe three years ago."

Hewey thought back. "Tall, skinny guy missing his left thumb?"

Sheets nodded. "Yes sir, that was Mister Dorn."

"What happened to him?"

"A horse fell on him and broke his leg. He was way off by himself. It was wintertime, and a norther come in. They said it looked like he tried to crawl, but he was dead when they found him."

"Damn." The thought saddened Hewey. Accidents often befell those in the cowboy trade, some of them deadly. The older Hewey grew, the more difficult it became for him to not dwell on the tragic accounts he heard.

"Then," Sheets went on, "just a couple weeks ago we shared our supper with a long-haired feller a little younger than me, name of Baca. He was headed north as we was comin' south, and we met him on the road one evening. That night he told us about you backin' him in some sorta bet at San Angelo."

Hewey smiled, remembering. "That boy was a hell of a horseman."

"He didn't say so, but I kinda got the idea he might be," said Sheets. "I got sort of a strange feelin' from him. I can't really describe it. It's sorta like when you can't quite think of somebody's name, but almost. You know what I mean?"

Hewey did know what Sheets meant. He remembered a similar feeling back when he had met Baca, a faint nagging in the back of his mind that would not quit.

Wes Wheeler had grown tired of the conversation.

The Blessing

"We best be moving along, fellers."

Hewey was not done, so he ignored Wheeler. "What are you boys doin' down here, anyhow? You're a long way from home."

Sheets grinned. "We're headed down to the Big Bend country. We heard they still got mustangs down there along the border, free for the takin' if a man can catch 'em. We figure to get us a herd of 'em put together and drive it back to the Panhandle. We'll break 'em along the way, and by the time we get home we'll have us a herd of broke ponies, ready to sell. Easy money."

The other boys were nodding in agreement, full of youthful excitement at the adventure ahead. Hewey knew their plan would come with more hardships than they seemed to realize, but he thought it could work. There would be no easy money in it, though.

A faraway look came over Hewey's face as he remembered. "Me and Snort Yarnell caught some mustangs down in Mexico a few years back, sort of north of Muzquiz. That's not too far from where you're headed. We didn't make much money when it was all over, but dern it was fun. I sure wish I could pack up and go with you."

Sheets perked up at the mention of Hewey coming along. "We'd sure be glad to have you, Mister Calloway."

The faraway look slowly left Hewey's face as reality returned. "I wish I could, but I got obligations keepin' me here, I reckon." He nodded at Wheeler. "The sheriff here has me under arrest right this minute, to tell you the truth."

Sheets looked from Hewey to Wheeler uncertainly. "I can't tell if you're just messin' with us."

"It's true. I'm a known outlaw."

Sheets decided there was a joke afoot. He smiled. "You want us to bust you loose?"

Wheeler placed his hand on the butt of his pistol, and Sheets' eyes grew wide. Hewey said, "Take it easy, Wes. They're just kids."

That seemed to hurt Sheets' pride, but he said nothing. Wheeler looked at Hewey, resolute in his impatience. "Enough, Hewey. We got to be movin' along."

Hewey turned to Sheets. "You boys be careful down there. You get into trouble, find the Circle W, south of Alpine. Tell Aparicio Rodriguez I sent you. He'll take care of you."

"Thank you, Mister Calloway. I'm sure we'll be fine. It's sure been an honor to meet you."

Wes Wheeler led off, and Hewey reluctantly followed. The young cowboys all nodded at him as they passed. Hewey thought back to all the years he had lived as they were, carefree and unburdened. It seemed like a lifetime ago. A wave of melancholy swept over him. Head down, he stared at the black mane of the dun horse as they rode along in silence.

Chapter Thirteen

Although Upton City did not have a judge in residence, it did have a courthouse. The building was small, as far as courthouses go, but Upton County only held a few hundred residents, at most. The courthouse was two stories, built of light-colored rock, with the sheriff's office and small jail located at the rear of the building.

As they neared the courthouse, Wes Wheeler conversationally told Hewey that there was talk of moving the county seat to Rankin, and he feared that might come to pass.

The location of county seats held little interest for Hewey. Still, he wondered briefly what that might mean for his ranch, being close as it was to the town of Rankin.

"If they move it, I reckon you wouldn't have to ride as far to come arrest me next time you get some bogus charge against me."

Wheeler looked pained. "Dammit, Hewey, you know that ain't fair. I'm just doin' my job."

"That may be, but you know as well as I do that Fat Gervin is a lying son of a bitch."

"I'll grant you that," Wheeler said. "But the fact is that somebody shot him. If it wasn't you, then who was it?"

"Hell, I don't know." Hewey was exasperated. "Fat's cheated half the folks in this county. You got a whole list of suspects. I can't figure why you chose me."

Wheeler did not answer. They had ridden to the rear of the courthouse, to the door with a faded wooden sign above it that simply said SHERIFF. A lone horse stood hipshot outside.

Both Hewey and Wheeler studied the horse, although for different reasons. Hewey admired the horse itself, a pretty dappled gray with a short back, wide hip and a pretty head. Wheeler knew the horse was nice, but his eyes went to the saddle, and particularly the scabbard tied on the right side. The stock of what appeared to be a Winchester rifle protruded from it. It had not been too many years earlier that everyone carried a rifle on their saddle. Those days were fading fast.

Wheeler led the way inside, where they found a man sitting in a chair with his back to the wall. Wheeler got the impression the man had been watching them through the window as they arrived.

The man stood as they entered. He was perhaps sixty years old, his tanned face clean shaven. He was small, several inches shorter than Hewey, and slight of build. He wore tan pants tucked into tall-topped boots, and on his white shirt was a silver peso someone had crudely cut into a badge. Piercing blue eyes touched on Hewey, then moved to Wheeler.

Hewey could feel an intensity coming off the lawman, and he began to worry the little man had come for him.

"You would be Sheriff Wheeler?" asked the man. He spoke quietly, his voice almost monotone.

Wheeler held out his hand, which the man took in his own. "I'm Wes Wheeler."

The man replied. "I'm Clarence Rogers, Captain of Company E of the Texas Rangers. I got a message from an old friend of mine, asking for help in your county. I came here first, as a courtesy, and also to ask where to find him."

It seemed to Hewey that he had heard that name before, but it did not click immediately.

"Who's your friend, the one asking for the help?" asked Wheeler.

"He's a retired Ranger. Name of Hanley Baker."

Wheeler and Hewey exchanged a surprised glance that was not lost on Rogers. "What?" the man asked.

"I don't know what Hanley Baker asked you to help him with, but I met Mister Baker earlier today. This here is Hewey Calloway. He's a friend of Baker."

Hewey stuck out his hand. "I sure am glad you come."

Rogers shook hands. "You're the one havin' trouble with a banker welshing on a real estate deal, ain't you? Well, I don't see how I can help much with that, but me and Hanley go way back. We done some fightin' together in the old days. That sort of thing means a lot to me, so I come anyway."

The lawman still spoke quietly, almost without emotion. Hewey got the feeling he would do best to stay on Rogers' good side. "Well, sir, things have got a little more complicated now. Wes here arrested me earlier today."

Surprise showed briefly on Rogers' face. He had no tolerance for criminals and would not waste his time assisting this one. "Arrested you? For what?"

"Hell if I know," answered Hewey. "Wes, what're you chargin' me with, anyhow?"

Wheeler was not too sure of that himself. "Attempted murder, I reckon."

Rogers stared from one to the other. "Gentlemen, I believe I should hear the entire story, if you don't mind."

Hewey and Wheeler took turns telling the story, which seemed natural to them but struck Rogers as an oddity. In all his years as a Texas Ranger, he had never seen a man charged with attempted murder sit in the sheriff's office, unrestrained, and tell his story alongside the man who had arrested him. That the sheriff was not intimidated by Hewey Calloway, and likely even thought him innocent, became more and more apparent.

They had just finished their telling of the story, which they mostly agreed upon, when the exterior door was pushed open, and Hanley Baker stepped inside.

"Took you long enough," Hewey said. "I been

wastin' away here."

"I can tell it's goin' hard for you," replied Baker.

Clarence Rogers stood, and he and Baker shook hands warmly. Decades earlier, the two men had seen and even done some things that both wished they had not, but those events had formed a deep bond between the tough men. They did not speak of it, but it was there.

Baker said, "It's sure good to see you, Clarence. I wasn't even sure you got my message."

"Sorry it took so long. Two dumb farm boys had been goin' around robbin' little stores and cafes around Midland. Wasn't a big deal 'til one of them whacked a store owner with a piece of pipe. Damned near killed the old man." Rogers sighed. "So, I had to stay hooked 'til I got that sorted out."

Rogers had been talking to Baker, but Wheeler interrupted. "I got a poster on them last week. It said they might head this way. You arrested those boys?"

The Ranger turned and looked at Wheeler. He was not certain he liked the sheriff. There were only a handful of people he *did* like. "I arrested one of them. But neither will be causin' any more trouble."

Wheeler opened his mouth to ask what that meant, but Rogers' meaning hit him before he spoke. Rogers seemed untroubled by it all. Wheeler had never fired his gun during all his years as a sheriff, and Rogers' cold casualness chilled him.

Rogers said to Baker, "I wasn't too sure what I

could do on the cattle deal. I wouldn't even have come if it wasn't you that asked. But this deal," he pointed vaguely at Hewey, "this makes it my business."

Baker said, "I'd like to help you, what little I can."

"Be glad to have you, long as the sheriff doesn't mind."

Rogers really did not care one way or the other if the sheriff minded, but he had found that politeness often went a long way, even when it was insincere. Wheeler remembered his earlier warning to Baker to stay out of it, but he looked at Rogers and decided not to press the issue. "I welcome any help either of you can give."

Baker smiled faintly. Rogers asked him, "So you've known Calloway here a long time?"

"Not as long as I've known you, but yeah, I know him. We rode all the way to Wyoming together, got in a couple of little scrapes along the way."

Rogers' eyebrows raised slightly. He asked, "And you don't think he did the shootin'?"

"Hell, Clarence, I was with him when it happened. I *know* he didn't do it."

The look Rogers gave Wheeler withered the younger, larger man, but Wheeler still countered, if weakly. "Ranger, you got to understand. The man who was shot, Mister Gervin, he has a lot of influence around here. He claims Hewey shot him. I can't ignore that."

Rogers did not deign to argue. He had always

thought it was a waste of time to argue with those he felt beneath him, which was a considerable crowd. "Where is this Mister Gervin now?"

"He's at his house, the one here in town. You can't miss it. It's the biggest house in Upton City, up at the north end. I sent for his wife at the ranch. I reckon she'll be there takin' care of him. Plus, the doctor is checking in."

Rogers walked out the door without a word. Baker paused, looking at Hewey. "We'll get this figured out pretty soon. Clarence ain't one to mess around." To the sheriff, he said, "Take care of ol' Hewey here. Make sure nobody lynches him before we get back."

"This ain't no time for jokes," Hewey said.

Baker kept a somber expression. "Who's jokin'?"

A surly voice from somewhere inside the house answered their knock on the front door, demanding to know who was there. Clarence Rogers had no patience for those who insisted on talking to him through doors. The knob turned in his hand, and he opened the door and stepped inside. "Texas Rangers," he said loudly. The nicely furnished living room was empty of life.

"You can't just come in here," the voice demanded from down a hallway.

Rogers followed the voice, and Baker followed him down a short hall and into a bedroom. They found a large, soft man lying on a bed wearing only the white pants from his pajamas. His bald head shone, the strips of hair meant to cover it hanging loosely over his ear. A white bandage covered his right side, a few inches above where his belt would be, if he had been wearing one.

Rogers frowned distastefully at the scene. "You are Frank Gervin?"

Fat Gervin was belligerent. "You got no right to just come in here uninvited."

Rogers stepped to the bed and roughly sat on the edge. The mattress shifted, despite his small frame, and the movement made Fat groan. Rogers stared at him, and Fat could not hold the gaze. In his quiet, monotone voice, Rogers said, "I am Clarence Rogers, with the Texas Rangers, although I'm certain you heard me say that already." Rogers paused and looked at Gervin for a long moment. "We are looking into the shooting. I need you to tell me what happened. Be exact."

Fat thought about it for several seconds before he began. He told them he had been there alone, just after dark, when someone knocked on the front door. He never took visitors that late, he said, but he opened the door to find Hewey Calloway standing on the porch holding a pistol in his hand.

"He was drunk. I could tell. He was swaying back and forth, and he kept pointing that pistol at me. He told me I had cheated him on a land contract, which I in fact did not. Then he shot me."

Rogers stared at Fat. "That's it?"

"Well," Fat said uncertainly. "I was laying there on the floor, afraid he was going to shoot me again. Hewey Calloway looked down at me and said, 'That's what you get, Frank.'"

"Nothing more?" asked Rogers, his steady gaze still unnerving Fat.

"That's all I can remember," Fat whined. "I don't feel well. Please, I need to rest."

Baker spoke for the first time. "Where's your wife?"

Fat's puffy fingers fidgeted. "She's at the ranch, I suppose."

"She didn't come to check on you?" Baker asked.

"I'm sure she's busy with our children."

Rogers stood, causing another groan from Fat. "I feel like we'll need to talk more."

"Wait!" said Fat, before they left. "Did Wes Wheeler arrest Hewey Calloway? I told him I wanted that son of a bitch in the jail."

Rogers turned and stared at Fat, then turned and walked out the door. Outside, he told Baker, "I did not care for that man."

"From what I understand, not many do, other than those that can get somethin' from him. Before we go anywhere else, let's go back to the jail. I want you to hear somethin'."

Rogers looked at his friend quizzically, but Baker offered no explanation. They stepped on their horses, which had been tied to the white wooden fence surrounding the Gervin house.

They found Hewey still sitting in the outer office rather than a cell. He had his feet propped up and was reading the local newspaper. Wes Wheeler sat at his desk, and he pretended to be busy when Baker and Rogers walked into the room.

"Clarence, I want you and the sheriff to hear this," Baker said. "Hewey, what's the name of the man you supposedly shot?"

Hewey stared at Baker for several seconds, confused. He wondered where the question could be leading. "What the hell you talkin' about? Y'all left here twenty minutes ago to go see him. It's Fat Gervin."

Baker ignored him. He asked Rogers, "What did Gervin just tell us Hewey said, after he shot him?"

Rogers thought for a moment. "He said, 'That's what you get.'"

"There was something else."

A pause, then Rogers said, "That's what you get, Frank."

"That's right," Baker said. "I've been around Hewey for the last week or so, and he's spent half of it bitchin' about this banker Gervin. Not once did he call him Frank. It's always Fat this, or Fat that. Never Frank."

"That's all I ever called him, far back as I can remember. At first it was sort of a joke, but then it just sorta stuck."

The Blessing

The frown on Rogers face deepened. "Thou shall not bear false witness. That's the ninth commandment. I have no use for a liar."

Hewey wondered what Rogers thought about the other commandments. He couldn't remember which one it was, but he knew there was one that said something about not killing people. Maybe Rogers had missed that one.

Rogers asked quietly, "Sheriff, is this enough to convince you?"

Wheeler squirmed in his chair. "Sir, I'm not the one needs convincin'. I sent a message to the district judge. I think we best wait for him. I don't think Hewey did it, but we still got a wounded man who says Hewey shot him."

Moving toward the door, Rogers said, "If I keep lookin', I'm liable to find enough rope to hang this Frank Gervin. Just so you know."

A small smile came over Hewey's face. He was feeling better about his situation all the time. "Better make it a stout rope," he advised. "Else it'll never hold all that weight."

Chapter Fourteen

Clarence Rogers and Hanley Baker left early the next morning, their horses following a two-rut wagon road that Wes Wheeler had said would take them to the Two Cs Ranch. They had taken the time before they left to eat breakfast in the cafe below the small hotel where they had both stayed.

Neither man had a definite idea what they were hoping to learn at the ranch, but they felt like it was the logical next step. It was also the only thing they could think of doing just then. They were curious why Doreen Gervin had chosen not to visit her husband, but they had little idea what else they might learn from the woman.

They had seen no traffic whatsoever on the road, until about midmorning when a dusty automobile approached them. Rogers and Baker moved their horses to the side of the road and stopped, in what they felt was the universal sign that the approaching vehicle should also stop. It was common courtesy.

The automobile never slowed. As it passed, the men saw briefly through the side window the figure of a woman. She stared straight ahead, not giving them a moment's glance. They both stared at the retreating vehicle. It was not common for women to drive automobiles.

"You don't reckon that was her, do you?" asked Baker.

"I don't know what she looks like, do you?"

"Never seen her," said Baker.

"I get the feelin' that was her. But, we've come this far. We might as well go on and check."

It was late morning when they reached the headquarters of the Two Cs. There was no one in sight, not at the main house nor around the barns or bunkhouse. The large main house was set apart from the other buildings. They knocked on its front door. There was no answer.

It was only a couple hundred yards to the other buildings, but Rogers and Baker remounted their horses rather than walking. They never considered doing otherwise.

Connected to the bunkhouse was a small kitchen. Inside, they found a sloppy, overweight man smoking a cigarette as he prepared what appeared to be biscuits. He looked over at them with impassiveness.

"Mornin'," said Baker.

The man grunted in reply, then went back to his work.

"We're lookin' for Doreen Gervin," Rogers said testily.

The cook looked at Rogers for a couple seconds, dwelling on the badge, and decided it might be in his best interest to be more cooperative. "She was up there last night. I heard that automobile earlier, but I didn't go look. It was probably her leavin', but I don't know for sure."

"Who you cookin' dinner for," Baker asked. "I don't see nobody."

"The hands are comin' in for dinner today. They're workin' just a little way out." The cook gestured with his chin toward the south.

Baker asked, "Reckon when they'll be in?"

In answer, the cook looked at the back wall, where a dusty clock hung crookedly. It showed the time to be a quarter to noon.

"We'll wait," Baker said, and they walked outside and sat in a couple wooden chairs, in the shade of the porch.

"I ain't got much patience for dirty cooks with bad attitudes," said Rogers.

"Clarence," Baker said. "You didn't have much patience for anything thirty years ago, and it seems you may have lost some of that."

Ten minutes later they watched a line of horsemen trotting toward the headquarters. They had little hope of learning anything from the men about the shooting, but they had decided they might also ask a question or two about the cattle deal on Hewey's ranch.

Baker crossed one leg over the other, grunting quietly at the discomfort the move produced in his knee. "Maybe they'll invite us to stay for dinner."

"You'd eat what that nasty cook sets out?"

The Blessing

"I've ate a lot worse, and so have you," Baker said. "I was there many times."

Rogers replied, "Well, I got smarter."

The cowboys rode to the saddle house first. Rogers and Baker sat and watched them unsaddle their horses and turn them loose in a corral made of cedar posts. The men obviously meant to trade mounts before heading out again. Several of the men eyed the strangers warily, in a fashion with which Rogers and Baker were familiar. It was the look of a man who had spotted a lawman and wanted no part of him.

A couple of them appeared as if they did not even want to come eat, but in the end, they decided that would look suspicious. All six of them filed toward the porch, where Baker and Rogers stood waiting. The man in the lead looked at them with a touch of hostility. He was slender, middle-aged, with light red hair and a red tint to his face.

Burgin Stamp's eyes had a look that Rogers and Baker had seen before in men who often made foolish and occasionally violent decisions. Baker had pondered this many times, and all he could come up with was that a certain type of craziness showed itself in the eyes.

"Can I help you with somethin'?" Stamp asked, in a tone meant to show he held no inclination whatsoever to provide any sort of assistance.

Rogers bristled. "My name is Clarence Rogers. I'm a captain with the Texas Rangers. What's your name, son?"

Stamp did not like being called son. He narrowed his eyes at Rogers. "Burgin Stamp. I'm the wagon boss here."

"Who's the foreman?" Rogers asked him.

Stamp and one other man carried pistols, which had never been too common among regular working cowboys and had become extremely rare over the last twenty years. The other armed man stood a step behind and two steps to the side of Stamp. Three of the men stood nearby, unarmed and uncertain.

The eldest of the cowboys walked to the porch and sat on the edge, silently showing his separation from the group. Stamp shot him a look of contempt, which was returned in kind.

Stamp told Rogers, "Foreman is the owner. Frank Gervin. He ain't here."

"I know he ain't here. He's in town. Someone shot him."

The look of surprise on Stamp's face was genuine, in Rogers' opinion. He had begun to wonder if the man might have been responsible, although he had not figured out why Stamp would have done it, other than pure meanness. Stamp seemed to have plenty of that.

Rogers asked anyway. "Any of you boys know anythin' about that?"

Several shook their heads side to side, but only Stamp spoke. "Hell, mister, ain't nobody here thinks Gervin is his friend, but none of us has any call to shoot him."

Rogers tended to believe him, although in his experience, men like Stamp often lied even when the truth would work better.

"All right. I got another question for you fellers. Frank Gervin sold part of this ranch. The south end of it. There is a legal dispute concerning the cattle that went with it not matching the description in the contract. Any of you know anythin' at all about that?"

Two of the unarmed men behind Stamp exchanged a brief, worried look. Rogers saw it. He said, "You boys don't want any part of this. You best tell me."

"There ain't nothin' to tell," Stamp snapped, still looking at Rogers.

One of the men looked at the ground. The other looked from Rogers to Baker nervously.

From the edge of the porch, the old cowboy who had separated himself looked at Rogers. Durwood Todd said quietly, "I can tell you a little about that, Ranger."

"Keep your mouth shut, old-timer," said Stamp, shooting an acid look at Todd.

Rogers' left hand was moving while Stamp was still speaking. He had run out of patience. He delivered an open-handed slap across Stamp's face. The blow cracked like a whip. Stamp was stunned. No one had slapped him since his mother had last done it fifteen years earlier, and that had been for cussing.

"You old son of a," Stamp did not finish because

Rogers slapped him again, harder this time.

Rogers had always enjoyed slapping rude criminals. He felt the act accurately demonstrated his contempt. This was not lost on Stamp. Outraged, he reached for the pistol on his hip. Stamp had been a part-time criminal and full-time bully since adolescence, but he was no gunfighter. The anger that coursed through him did nothing for his dexterity.

He had only touched the butt of his pistol when Rogers slapped him again, this time with the barrel of his own revolver. Stunned, Stamp slowly slumped to his knees. He looked up at Rogers just in time to see the Ranger's small boot kick him square in the mouth.

The cowboy nearest to Stamp, the one with the pistol, had watched in shock as the small Ranger methodically dismantled Stamp, and with such ease. Stamp was thought to be a tough man. The Ranger was looking down at Todd, not paying attention to the other man. The cowboy wondered for a second what he should do.

"Don't," said a voice from the porch.

The man looked up to see the other old man pointing a big pistol at him. The cowboy raised his hands slightly, no longer in the fight.

"Drop it on the ground," Baker said.

"I wasn't plannin' to do anythin'. Honest," said the man, dropping his gun and stepping away from it.

"Sure you weren't," Baker said.

Rogers had produced a pair of handcuffs from a

pocket, and he locked the unconscious Stamp's hands behind his back. He looked around at Baker. "I don't believe this man was as tough as he thought."

"They rarely are," said Baker.

Looking back toward the cowboys, Rogers asked politely, "Would one of you fellers mind saddlin' a horse for this man? He's goin' with us, and I don't think he'll be able to do it himself."

"I'll do it," said Durwood Todd, rising from the edge of the porch. "I'm comin' with you, too. I should've left here a long time ago."

It took half an hour for Todd to saddle a horse for himself, another for Stamp, and then to gather his few belongings. It only took a few minutes for Stamp to come to his senses. He stared at Rogers with silent hatred.

Baker, who was still less concerned about the cook's cleanliness than was Rogers, came out of the small kitchen with a couple cups of coffee and two plates. Rogers accepted the coffee but declined the plate.

Stamp's mouth was still dribbling blood, but Baker offered the plate to him anyway. Stamp did not move or reply.

When Todd brought up the horses, Rogers told him to get something he could eat while traveling, because they were leaving. He hoisted Stamp to his feet and led him to the extra horse Todd had brought. Stamp could not mount without assistance, not with his hands cuffed behind his back. When Rogers tried to help, Stamp resisted.

Quietly, so only Stamp could hear, Rogers told him, "You get on this horse right now, or I'll stomp on you until you decide to. Then, when we get out of sight of your friends here, I'll shoot you in the stomach and say you was tryin' to escape. You'll die, but it will take a while, and it'll hurt like hell the whole time."

Stamp said nothing, and he looked at Rogers as if he were trying to gauge the man's sincerity. Rogers told him, "I been doin' this longer'n you been alive, boy, since the days when the law was just as likely to shoot a piece of trash like you as take him to town. Old habits are hard to break, especially when a man don't even want to break them. Now get on the goddamned horse."

Stamp got on the horse. He remained sullen and silent, but he gave no more trouble. Rogers led Stamp's horse behind his own, and they struck an easy trot toward town.

Durwood Todd became talkative after a few minutes. He told them in detail how the Two Cs hands had pushed all the cattle that were on the old Simmons place to the boundary fence and then sorted them there. The nicer cattle went north and the Longhorns stayed there. Then they did the same on the Two Cs, pushing enough Longhorns south to make the count right.

The Blessing

"It took damn near three weeks to get it all done," Todd said. "We had hell pairing up all them cows with the right calves. Some of them we never did get right. I reckon some of them calves starved out there, unless they was able to crawl through the fence and find their mammies."

Todd pointed at Stamp with his chin. "This son of a bitch, he don't care about that. He ain't got a lick of kindness in him. I don't reckon Mister Gervin does neither. I've known him since he first went to work for ol' C.C. Tarpley, all them years ago. You never met a more counterfeit son of bitch, I guarantee you."

Baker and Rogers acknowledged that they held similar feelings toward the man. Baker told him about Fat Gervin claiming Hewey shot him. Todd was shocked, then indignant.

"Hell, Hewey wouldn't shoot nobody 'less they damned sure deserved it. He's a little bit foolish now and then, but he ain't mean," Todd said. "Hewey's a good ol' boy."

"Why did you stay on at the Two Cs, if things were so bad?" Rogers wanted to know.

"Look at me. I'm an old man. Nobody wants to hire an old cowpuncher. I was scared I couldn't find no other job if I left there. But I damn sure wanted to leave, ever' since ol' C.C. died."

"You ain't that old, probably about the same as me and Hanley."

Todd raised his eyebrows, looking from one to the

other. "You boys ain't exactly spring chickens yourself."

Baker thought about it. "I can't speak for Hewey, but I do know he's shorthanded. When this deal is over, you might ought to go and talk to him."

It was late afternoon when they reached the jail. They found Hewey sitting in the sheriff's chair with his feet propped up on the desk, drinking a beer that had evidently been provided by his friend Dutch Schneider, who sat across from him. The pair were laughing as Rogers pushed Burgin Stamp through the door, followed closely by Baker. Durwood Todd had remained outside.

Baker and Rogers looked over the situation momentarily. Baker said, "What in the hell, Hewey?"

Hewey was genuinely perplexed. "What?" he asked.

"Me and Clarence are out here ridin' all over Upton County, tryin' to get you out of jail, while you're sittin' here drinkin' beer."

"Well, I'd go with you, but Wes won't let me leave. He said I can do whatever I please, long as I stay right here. So, I'm doin' as I please."

Rogers pushed Stamp into the jail's one cell. Baker said, "Well, you got a roommate now."

"Doesn't matter to me. I don't sleep in there," Hewey said. "It smells bad."

"Where is the sheriff?" asked Rogers.

"Think he went for coffee. He didn't want any

beer."

Baker said, "We didn't find anything to help with your shootin' case, but we got a good witness who'll testify that Fat Gervin changed the cattle before you took possession of the ranch. Looks to me like it should be enough to get that deal sorted out."

Hewey began grinning. That news, mixed with the two beers he had drank, raised his spirits. He was about to ask who the witness was when Tommy Calloway cautiously stepped into the sheriff's office. The small room was practically full of men.

"Tommy!" Hewey exclaimed happily.

Tommy was serious. "Uncle Hewey, Mister Baker, I got someone y'all need to talk to. It's real important."

"Who is it, son?" asked Baker.

Tommy stepped out, then quickly reappeared followed by Leta, the girl he had been seeing. Behind her, timidly, came the blonde teller from the bank. Hewey was the only one to recognize them, other than perhaps Dutch Schneider.

Pointing at the blonde, Tommy said, "This here is Patsy Gibson. She works for Fat Gervin, up at the bank. She's got somethin' to tell, about Fat gettin' shot."

They all stared at her. In a tone far gentler than any of them were accustomed to hearing from him, Rogers asked, "What is it, young lady?"

Patsy seemed near tears. "I was there," she said.

Chapter Fifteen

They all stared in shocked silence at Patsy, who stared at the floor. Finally, Hanley Baker said, "Tommy, would you mind steppin' out and finding the sheriff? I think it might be best if he hears this." He turned his gaze to Leta. "Miss, what's your role in this?"

"She's, uh, with me," Tommy said. "Patsy told Leta what happened, and she told me. That's how all this came about."

Rogers, still with the kind tone, said to Leta, "Thank you for the help, but it might be better for you to go on home now."

Leta let out a relieved breath, although Patsy appeared as if she might prefer her to stay. The two had never been particularly close, but Leta was the nearest thing she had to a friend.

Tommy led Leta out the door, then stuck his head back in. "Mister Wheeler is comin'. Uncle Hewey, I'm goin' to tell Spring about this. She's at the hotel."

"Thank you, Tommy." Hewey felt like dancing, even though he wasn't any good at it. If this girl was there when Fat was shot, then she had to know he had not been.

Wes Wheeler walked in and surveyed the crowd in his small office, his gaze lingering momentarily on Dutch Schneider and then on Hewey, who was sitting behind the desk with a beer bottle in his hand. His attention turned to Patsy Gibson, whom he knew only in passing.

"Is anyone goin' to tell me what's happenin' here?" Wheeler felt like he had lost control. He felt like cussing but held back out of respect for the girl.

Hewey pointed his bottle at the girl and said happily, "This is Patsy. She works for Fat. She come to clear my name."

Wheeler eyed Patsy skeptically, but she nodded her head at him. The sheriff turned to Schneider. "Dutch, I get the feelin' we're fixin' to talk about some things you ought not hear. Might be time for you to go."

Schneider had hoped to stay and listen, but he put up no argument. Testily, Wheeler told him, "And take the beer with you."

The barman stood and gathered the beer. When Wheeler looked away, he slid another bottle across the desk to Hewey, who grinned and winked at him.

Wheeler looked toward the single cell in the back and saw Stamp sitting on the cot, watching and listening. The sheriff frowned. "Who in the hell is that?" he asked, forgetting not to cuss.

"Long story," said Rogers. He stepped across the room and shut a wooden door, so Stamp could not hear. "Let's talk to this young lady first." He turned to Patsy. His tone was still uncharacteristically friendly. "You said you were there when Frank Gervin was shot."

Her voice was quiet, frightened even. "Yes, sir."

"Who shot him?" Rogers asked gently.

Patsy looked at Wheeler, then back at Rogers. "His wife."

Rogers raised his eyebrows, and Hewey let out a long, slow whistle that tapered off at the end. Rogers asked, "This was at Frank Gervin's house?"

"Yes," Patsy said.

"Start at the beginning. What happened?"

Patsy took a deep breath, as if steeling herself. "I heard someone rattle the doorknob. I guess Mister Gervin had locked it. He didn't act like he wanted to open it, but he walked toward the door anyway. I guess Mrs. Gervin had a key, because the door opened all of a sudden. I could tell she was already mad. She looked at him and then me, and then she pulled out a little gun and just shot him. She never said a word. Just turned around and left. I was scared to death she was goin' to come back and shoot me, so I ran out the back door and home."

Baker was leaning against the wall near the door. "Why did you wait so long to say somethin'? You had to know Hewey was on the hook for it."

Patsy looked at Baker, then gave Hewey an apologetic look. Tears leaked from her eyes. "I'm sorry, Mister Calloway. I was scared to say anything. I'm twenty-two years old. I was in my boss's house after dark. A married man. You know how that looks."

They did know how that looked, and she saw it on

their faces. "I never did anything, um, well, physical, with Mister Gervin. I just sort of flirted with him, and he kept giving me little raises on my paycheck. I hated it, though. You've got to believe that."

All four men looked at the young, attractive girl, and they had no problem believing she did in fact hate it. Yet she still had done it.

Baker said, "But you were in his house, late in the evening."

"That was the first time," she said, somewhat unconvincingly.

"All that really doesn't matter here," Rogers said. "As long as you're certain it was Doreen Gervin who did the shootin'."

"Yes, sir. I'm sure. She'd been at the bank before, several times, always acting like she hated me and Leta both." Patsy looked to Hewey. "You got to know. Leta's a good girl. She made it clear to Mister Gervin right off that she wouldn't tolerate anything from him."

Hewey nodded his thanks. He saw no reason to tell her that he saw the difference between the two of them the first time he saw them at the bank.

Rogers looked to Wes Wheeler. "I think we saw Mrs. Gervin headed to town earlier. Have you seen her?"

"I saw two automobiles outside their house here earlier today," Wheeler said. "She was there then, if she ain't left."

"That's a big thing to have two automobiles, for

just one family, ain't it?" asked Baker.

Wheeler said, "They only had one up until just a few months ago, then they bought a new one. That was just about the time they started sellin' off parts of her daddy's ranch."

"I'm goin' down there right now," Rogers said.

Baker said nothing, but he moved toward the door. Rogers nodded his acceptance.

Wes Wheeler sighed, then stood. "I'll let you do the talkin', but I figure I ought to be there, at least."

"You been stayin' out of it all along, on account of public favor. I don't much like that, but I can understand it some," said Rogers. "You sure you want to get in it now?"

"I don't *want* to," Wheeler said. "But I feel like I got to anyway."

Rogers understood. Hewey stood up like he was going, too.

Baker pointed his finger at Hewey. "Hell no. You're stayin' here. Sheriff Wheeler will put you in that cell if we need to."

"I just want to see Fat's fat face when y'all tell him you know he's been lyin'." Hewey paused. "And then I want to tell him to kiss my ass."

Rogers gave Hewey a hard look that needed no words. Hewey sat back down sadly. Baker looked at Hewey and shook his head side to side in an effort at reproach, but a slight smile betrayed him.

Wes Wheeler had a saddled horse tied in the shade

of a large mesquite behind the courthouse. Rogers' and Baker's horses stood sleepily at a wooden hitching rail. All three men mounted for the short ride to the Gervin house on the edge of town. Two black vehicles were parked outside when they arrived. One was the automobile the woman had been driving earlier that morning.

They recognized that same woman when she answered their knock a minute later. Doreen Gervin had taken after her mother as far as looks, although her recent aggression hinted at her father's temper. She was a plump woman with a sour expression on her pale face. *Living with Fat Gervin could turn a woman sour*, Baker thought, *while living with Doreen might turn a man philanderous.* Then he wondered if he had it backward.

Doreen kept one hand on the door, as if she were about to shut it in their faces. "Yes?" she asked, her hostility coming through with only one word.

"You are Doreen Gervin?" asked Rogers, although he knew she was.

Her hostility remained. "Yes."

"I am Clarence Rogers with the Texas Rangers. This is my associate, Hanley Baker. I assume you know Sheriff Wheeler."

Doreen Gervin made no move and gave no reply. Rogers' limited patience was waning. "Mrs. Gervin, we must speak with you. You can politely invite us in, or we can escort you down to the sheriff's office and speak there. One of your cowboys is already there. I'm not certain how you would feel about sharing a cell with him."

Doreen's nostrils flared. She gave it some thought, then stepped aside and motioned them into the house. Rogers and Wheeler walked on into the room, but Baker motioned Doreen to proceed him. She had already shot one man in that room. He did not intend to become the second.

Rogers said, "I would prefer to speak with you and your husband at the same time, at least in the beginning. Is he able to come in here, or should we go to him?"

"We might as well go in there," Doreen sighed. "It'll take too long to get him up and in here."

Baker again hung back, allowing the other three to file into the bedroom. Rogers stood beside the bed, while Doreen and Wheeler stood at the foot. There was one straight-backed wooden chair in the corner, but none chose to sit. Baker leaned against the doorframe.

Fat Gervin lay much as he had before, although his mood had darkened. He looked at each of them in turn, no welcome in his expression. His face was flushed, and beads of sweat covered his forehead. Baker wondered if his tension was caused by their presence, or that of his wife.

"What can I do for you gentlemen? I thought it

was all wrapped up." Fat's voice was laced with irritation and perhaps a bit of nervousness.

Rogers said, "We've looked into your shootin', and we found some holes in your story. I think you both know what I'm talkin' about."

Doreen and Fat each shot a look toward the other. Quickly, she said, "What are you talking about? What holes?"

"Well," said Rogers. "Mostly that you're the one who shot your husband and he lied to everyone about who really did it."

Doreen sank down into the lone chair. "That little whore. She told you, I suppose."

"We have a witness, yes ma'am," said Rogers.

Looking at Fat, Doreen hissed, "You said she wouldn't tell anyone."

Fat did not know what to say. He shrugged, then winced from the movement.

"Mrs. Gervin, we have a good case against you for attempted murder. Mister Gervin, I have you for lyin' to a law enforcement officer and filing a false report. You did sign a report, didn't you?"

Fat said nothing, so Rogers looked to Wes Wheeler. The sheriff nodded.

From the corner, Baker chimed in. "I believe Hewey Calloway would have a good shot at winnin' a defamation lawsuit. This has scarred his reputation, and I know for a fact that sittin' in jail has been damned near unbearable for him."

Doreen stared at them icily. Fat squirmed, as best he could in his present state. He said, "Gentlemen, I don't care to press charges against my wife. It was an unfortunate misunderstanding. That's all it was."

"Well, you see, Mister Gervin," Rogers said quietly. "I don't need you to press charges. The state of Texas will do that, whether you like it or not."

Doreen gave her husband a look like she wished she had killed him, rather than just wound him.

"Clarence," said Baker. "The law don't always make sense, does it? His charges are misdemeanors. Now Mrs. Gervin, hers is a felony. He'll only serve some local jail time, but she's headed for the penitentiary. But the way I see it, what he done is worse. I can't figure why he'd want to blame an innocent man. But I can see why she'd want to shoot him. That's easy to understand."

"I see your point," Rogers allowed. "I'm surprised it took her this long to shoot this counterfeit son of a bitch."

Doreen Gervin knew something extralegal was afoot. This was not normal law enforcement behavior, in her experience. She asked, "What are you getting at?"

Rogers told her they also had a witness who would testify that the Gervins knowingly exchanged the cattle before Hewey took possession of the land they sold to him. "I see no way you could win, should Hewey Calloway take you to civil court. That case looks as poor as your criminal cases. You folks are in tough shape."

Wes Wheeler had remained quiet until then, but he finally caught on. "Rangers, maybe there's a way we could all come to some sort of agreement here."

Baker acted as if the idea had never occurred to him. "It would save us all the hassle of havin' to testify. Probably be three different trials, if Hewey decides to sue these folks, and I'm sure he will. I'm gettin' too old for all that nonsense. I'd rather go fishin'."

Rogers looked from one Gervin to the other. "Do you two think you can agree on some sort of deal, given your recent … marital issues?"

"Ranger," Doreen said icily. "My husband likes to think he runs everything now. However, I am the one who inherited both the bank and the ranch. He'll do whatever I tell him." She gave her husband a look of contempt. "I believe he and I have a new understanding on that matter. So, basically, if I agree, then we both agree."

"Yes ma'am," said Rogers.

Two weeks later, a cool north wind was blowing across Upton County. It was one of those early cold fronts that ease into West Texas around the first of September, doing little to the temperature but giving a hint of cooler weather to come.

Hewey Calloway and Hanley Baker sat on their

horses, one on each side of a wire gate that separated Hewey's H bar C ranch and the Two Cs to the north of it. A long line of Hereford cows trailed between them, and Hewey and Hanley counted them as they passed. Fifty feet south of them, Tommy Calloway, Enrique Rodriguez and Durwood Todd quietly took their own counts.

Hewey had not necessarily needed the extra help, but the men wanted to come with him. He could not deny them the moment. They had all played their own roles in the events that had led to this.

There were seven cowboys on the Two Cs' side of the fence. Hewey did not recognize any of them, although most kept their distance.

As the last cow passed them, Hewey looked at Hanley, who smiled broadly and said, "Five hundred, exactly."

Hewey nodded. That was his count also. "Hanley, I'm overstocked now. I'll have to sell some of those old Longhorns to make room for these."

"Hell, just trail them down to Rankin and put them on a train for Fort Worth. The cattle business is so profitable that it'll only take you two, maybe three years to lose it all."

That brought a small smile to Hewey. He said, "You and Clarence Rogers got me a good deal. Too good, seems to me."

Baker thought about that for several seconds, looking off into the distance. He said, "People like those Gervins, they love money more'n anything. But when it came right down to it, I guess they loved themselves just a little bit more."

The other hands rode up to them. Enrique got off to shut the wire gate, and then they all headed south. The cows would scatter on their own.

Hewey asked Baker, "You and Samantha still leavin' tomorrow?"

"I reckon so." Baker and Samantha had postponed their departure until the cattle delivery took place. Baker wanted to see it through, and Clarence Rogers had asked him to stay until the end. The Ranger wanted a steady hand and sound mind there to head off any foolishness, from either side. Fortunately, there had been none.

Baker said, "I think I can convince her to stay in Texas, but it's goin' to have to be someplace east of here, where it rains more'n twice a year. She ain't used to this."

"I spent most of my life in this part of the country, and sometimes I don't know if I'm used to it."

"I'm thinkin' she'll like it around Fredericksburg or Kerrville," Baker said. "There's a spot on the Guadalupe River, just west of Kerrville, that's as perfect as any place you ever seen."

They reached a dim wagon trail that led toward headquarters, and they struck an easy trot down it. Hewey and Hanley rode side by side.

"I spent some time down around Kerrville. Pretty

place, but gettin' to be too many people."

"Yeah, but it's close enough to here that I can get back next time you get in trouble."

The bay colt Hewey was riding spooked at some danger only it could see. Hewey casually swatted the horse on the hip with one rein. "Shoot. I'm too old to get in any trouble."

Chapter Sixteen

Hewey had developed the habit of riding his perimeter fence every week or two. Occasionally, he would send Tommy or Enrique, but he preferred to look over things himself, when he could.

He liked to check the barbwire fence to make sure something, like a bull or even a feral hog, had not torn it up anywhere. The ride also gave him a chance to look at his country, typically only reaffirming his belief that it sure needed to rain some more.

The outer fence of the ranch stretched over twenty miles. Hewey always trotted most of it since he could not look things over closely at a lope and a walk was just too slow. If he selected a horse with a smooth trot, he could be home before dark without his leg aching too much.

One morning in early May, Hewey set off just after daylight. Tommy and Enrique had seemed happy to be sent off to work without him. They worked just as hard alone as when he was with them, but they had a little more fun along the way. Hewey knew all about that. It was not so long ago he had been the same.

The spring rains had been too scarce to suit anyone in Upton County, Hewey included. A few scattered showers had fallen, but it was not enough. It never was.

The old-timers all liked to tell how it had rained more in years past. Hewey never could tell if it was a change in the weather pattern or just a change in their memories. As far back as he could remember, Upton County had been too dry. Then again, if it rained all the time, the farmers would have moved in and plowed up all the grass.

Along the north fence, the one that marked the boundary between him and the Two Cs, Hewey encountered no one. That suited him. He intended to get along as best he could, but animosities were slow to fade. He was pleased to see no one had crossed from the Two Cs onto his land. That would have worried him.

A portion of Hewey's west fence was shared with an old man named Emil Becker. Hewey judged him to be a German by his accent and name, but he had never heard for certain. There were many Germans far to the southeast, around Fredericksburg, and Hewey figured Becker had probably originated somewhere around there.

Becker had four sections of land, a homestead place, and by all accounts he was a good cattleman. So, Hewey was surprised when he topped a brush-covered sandhill and saw several hundred goats covered in long, curly white hair. They were called Angora goats, Hewey knew. He had seen plenty of them in Central Texas, although he could not remember ever seeing any so far west. There were smaller herds of the hardy

Spanish goats scattered around, mostly owned by Mexican families, but not these Angora goats.

Becker was on the other side of the goats, and he began trotting toward Hewey on a fat flea-bitten gray. Becker was a small, thin man with blazing blue eyes. Sun-browned skin showed from under hair and beard that matched the color of his horse. Hewey had heard Becker had been a tough character in his youth, back when Upton County was barely settled, but that had been before Hewey's time. He only knew the man to be friendly.

"Howdy, Hewey," Becker said quietly as he rode up, stopping a few feet on the other side of the fence.

"Mornin', Mister Becker." Hewey waved his hand at the goats. "I didn't know 'til just now that you're in the goat business."

Becker frowned at the goats. "I got a nephew, lives down close to Mason, runs a couple thousand of them. He talked me into buying these. Said I could run a couple hundred on my little place and not have to sell any cows. He claims they eat different plants, so it don't matter."

Both men sat on their horses, silently staring at the goats, which were, in fact, moving about quickly, stopping here and there to browse on mesquite trees. They mostly ignored the grass preferred by cattle.

"I didn't believe it, not at first," said Becker. "But damned if it don't look like it might be true."

"How you plan to keep the coyotes out of them?"

Hewey asked. He knew enough about sheep and goats to know predation was a constant problem.

Becker scratched his beard, then kicked his gray horse in the side as it tried to lower its head to eat. "I ain't got that figured just yet. Been bringing them into a trap up by the house at night. Been workin' so far."

"That's what my brother Walter does with his sheep. Seems like an awful lot of work to me."

"Yep, damned sure is," agreed Becker.

The rancher looked across Hewey's pasture, noticing all the brush and mesquite trees. "I don't know, my young friend. A place as big as yours, you could run a couple thousand goats and not hurt your cattle at all. Might be somethin' to think about."

Hewey began to say something derogatory about goat ranchers, but he thought better of it. "I don't know, Mister Becker. I might just stick with cattle and horses."

The old man slowly turned his gray horse back toward his goats. "Suit yourself," he said. "But you change your mind, I'll set you up with my nephew. I'm sure he'd love to sell you some goats."

Hewey grinned to himself. *Goats*, he thought. *That'll be the day*. He eased Pincushion into a walk, studying the brush and short mesquite trees he passed. He pulled his horse to a stop with a slight movement of his hand, then turned and watched Becker's goats pruning the lower branches of the mesquites. *Goats*, he thought again.

The Blessing

The dirt road that led north from Rankin to Upton City ran alongside Hewey's east fence. There was never much traffic, since neither town was very large and neither offered much to those who did not have specific business in them.

Hewey made the corner and turned north along his eastern boundary, pleased that he had not found any major issues along his circle. When he neared the main entrance that led to the small headquarters, he saw a low-sided wagon turning into his gate. There were two sorrel horses pulling the wagon, with a stout buckskin horse tied behind. The buckskin looked familiar, but Hewey was still a quarter mile away and was not yet certain.

A man stepped down from the wagon and began opening the gate. As Hewey neared, he could see what appeared to be a woman sitting on the wagon's wooden seat. Familiarity grew, and Hewey pushed Pinchusion into a long trot that quickly closed the gap.

The first thing Hewey was certain of was the buckskin. The horse was named Chongo, and it belonged to Aparicio Rodriguez. Soon after that, he was close enough to see that it was indeed Aparicio at the gate, with Olivia sitting on the wagon seat, holding the lines. Little Elena sat in the bed of the wagon, just behind the seat, smiling broadly at Hewey from inside a barricade made of a couple soft suitcases, some pillows and Aparicio's saddle.

Elena was excited to see him, and she yelled his name as he approached. Hewey saw Olivia hold up a calming hand, seemingly admonishing Elena for something. Hewey was momentarily puzzled.

"Elena!" Hewey said happily. "What're you doing here?"

Olivia shot a look at her daughter, then answered for her. "We came to talk to you and Spring," she said cheerfully. "Where is my friend?"

"I reckon she's at the house," Hewey said. "I been gone all day, but she doesn't generally go too far without me."

Aparicio dragged the wire gate to the side, smiling as he did it. "You need a new gate, amigo. This one is no good for a big ranchero like you."

Hewey grinned but shook his head. "I reckon I understand a little better now why Old Man Jenkins and all them others were so tight with their money. I got a lot of land, some cows and a few good horses. But I don't have any more money than I did when I was drawin' wages."

Olivia drove the team through the gate and pulled them to a stop not far from Hewey, as Aparicio dragged the wire gate back and pulled it closed. "There are things more important than money, patron," she said pointedly.

Hewey looked at her curiously. Olivia was cheerful, happy even, but she was acting differently somehow, like something was on her mind. Hewey did not understand it, but then again, he had a long history of not understanding women. He let it go.

Aparicio climbed into the wagon and took the lines from his wife. He asked Hewey if he was ready, then clucked to the team. Aparicio held them to a walk, and they slowly made their way down the short road that led to the headquarters. Elena sat in the buggy, oddly quiet down inside her cocoon.

"How did you find me, anyhow?" Hewey asked.

"It was not so hard, my friend. I just asked around for the man with the new rancho, the gringo that probably falls off his horse most days 'cause he don't ride so good. Everyone I asked, they knew jus' who I am talking about. They pointed me here," Aparicio said.

Hewey snorted. "Shoot, I bet you just asked where to find the best-lookin' cowpuncher in Upton County, and they sent you straight here."

Aparicio studied Hewey closely, making a show of it. "No, my friend," he said with an overdone display of sadness. "I don't think they send me here for that one."

Spring was working in the new garden she had insisted they start. Hewey had resisted, due to his belief that a man was certain to receive a black mark and might even go straight to hell for plowing up good grass, even for a garden. In the end Spring had won, although the plowed area was smaller than she had initially proposed.

She began walking toward the house, and Hewey saw her smile broaden as she recognized the visitors. "Olivia! Aparicio!" she said excitedly, then her smile vanished, replaced with worry. "Where is Elena?"

Elena raised her head from behind the pillows that hid her. She grinned at Spring. "I'm just right here," the little girl said happily.

Relief washed over Spring, although Olivia was the only one to see it. Hewey stepped off Pincushion, loosened the cinch and dropped a rein over the hitching post. He helped Olivia step down from the wagon, then walked up to the horse nearest him and stood by it as Aparicio climbed down. Aparicio gave a quiet gracias before wrapping a rein to the same hitching post. The horses were tired and content to stand quietly.

"Did y'all just come to visit?" asked Spring happily. "How long are you staying?"

Olivia glanced at Aparicio, who only shrugged. She looked back at Spring. "I hope this is all right, but we brought you something." A pause as Olivia chose her words carefully. "You never talked about it, not to me, but women can see things. I could tell how sad you were, not having a family."

Spring did not answer. She was confused as to where this conversation was headed. Olivia walked to the wagon, leaned over the side and moved a couple of the suitcases that made up Elena's barricade. Aparicio reached over, picked up his daughter and held her.

The Blessing

Olivia picked up a small bundle, smiled at it, then turned and walked to Spring. "I wondered if we should ask you before just coming all this way, but there was no easy way," Olivia said. She held out the bundle toward Spring, who was already silently crying.

Hewey looked at the bundle, and shock pushed him back a step. Wrapped in the blanket was a tiny baby. The only thing showing was the small face. The baby's skin was pale brown, and a surprising amount of black hair showed from beneath a soft homemade hat. Spring carefully took the baby, tears streaming down her face.

"Her name is Eliza. If you want her, she is yours," Olivia said.

Spring stared down at the tiny face, unable to speak. Aparicio looked at Hewey and was only mildly surprised to see that his friend was crying also. Aparicio understood. Before Elena was born he might not have, but that had changed.

"We brought her for you. For both of you," Olivia went on.

Hewey was finally able to speak. "But where'd she come from?"

"From my cousin," Aparicio said. "She has many kids and not much money. Her husband left and did not come back. She did not think she could take care of another. We learned of this, and we thought of you and Spring."

Olivia was watching Spring, who remained silent.

"You don't have to take her, Spring. I'll keep her myself, but I felt I had to come here first. Something inside told me I should. I think perhaps it was God, that He sent me here."

Spring stared at the baby girl, who opened tiny brown eyes and looked up impassively. "Yes," Spring said quietly. She turned to Hewey, who nodded an approval that really did not matter to Spring. Her mind was already made up. "Of course, yes, we want her. I don't know what to say. Thank you."

Aparicio set Elena on the ground, then stepped over and hugged Hewey, who was not accustomed to hugging other men. The surprising embrace brought a flood of emotion from Hewey. He held back a sob, then began to cry almost as much as Spring. He could not have stopped it had he tried. Olivia watched, and she smiled approvingly.

Spring walked to the porch and sat in one of the rocking chairs, silently staring down at the tiny face that stared back at her. She had never seen anything so beautiful.

Their small house bustled with activity and visitors for nearly three weeks. The first night Hewey sent Tommy and Enrique to Walter's place to borrow a milk cow, which he knew Walter owned and he did not. The boys brought back the cow, along with Walter and

The Blessing

Eve.

Walter came and went over the next three weeks. Eve never left. Somehow Hewey stayed on her good side, mostly because he accepted all advice on caring for baby Eliza and because it was obvious to Eve that he was trying so hard to be a good father.

Cora Lawdermilk stayed three days straight before heading home, but afterward she returned every few days to visit. Spring was, in essence, a younger sister to her. Cora had never been able to bear children of her own, and she gladly fell into the role of doting aunt.

Spring would occasionally see the sadness and longing in Cora's eyes as she held Eliza. Spring knew the feeling all too well, and that there was little she could do for her friend.

Tommy and Enrique took up the slack for Hewey, who had a difficult time leaving Eliza for long. Tommy and Enrique had also grown very attached to the baby. They liked to stare at her, although they were awkward on the rare occasions when either of them felt comfortable enough to hold the baby. Enrique talked to her in quiet Spanish. Both thought of her as a little sister.

Hewey had never in his life felt the contentment that washed over him as he held his daughter, holding her tiny hands or stroking her fine black hair.

One evening Hewey sat and watched Spring feeding baby Eliza. It was a rare moment when they were alone. Everyone else was outside. Hewey stared at the little girl, at her brown skin and black hair. "Things will be different for us," he said. "And for her."

Spring knew what he meant, and she was quick to flare. "Because she's a Mexican?"

"Yes," he said softly. "You know there are some that won't like it. They'll say she should be raised by her own kind. I wish it weren't the case, but there are some folks who don't think like we do, not on this."

Regretful of her earlier tone, Spring said, "I know. I don't understand it, and I hate it's that way."

"It's goin' to be a battle at times. Some folks will say things we don't like. We'll have to fight."

"She's worth it," said Spring, looking at Eliza. "I'll fight them all."

The Rodriguez family stayed four days before heading back to the ranch south of Alpine. Olivia and Elena wanted to stay longer, but Aparicio felt obligated to get back to the Circle W. Morgan Jenkins had sanctioned the trip, but Aparicio felt certain Jenkins' approval had its limits. Hewey figured Aparicio was correct.

"Hewey," Aparicio said as they were leaving, still pronouncing it more like Hooey. "Little Eliza there, she come from Ojinaga, jus' like me and Elena, and Enrique. She got the blood. She gon' be a good little caballera. You'll see."

Hewey smiled, picturing it. He had already shown Biscuit to Eliza, although he figured she might need another month or two before she was riding much. She was still only a few days old, he reasoned.

Spring and Olivia both cried during the goodbyes. Elena hugged both Spring and Hewey, as did Olivia. Aparicio hugged Spring, then turned and held out a hand to Hewey.

"I can't thank you enough, all of you," Hewey said, shaking Aparicio's hand.

"Thanks are not necessary, my friend. We know ya'll gon' take care of that little girl. That's all we need," said Aparicio.

They were still shaking hands, and Hewey suddenly pulled Aparicio toward him and wrapped his arms around the other man, holding him a few seconds before letting go.

"Gracias, amigo," Hewey said quietly.

"De nada," answered Aparicio.

The month of May brought an unusual amount of rain for Upton County, and by June the grass had greened up and here and there small pockets of yellow and purple wildflowers colored the landscape.

Hewey slowly began working more, but he left later and returned much earlier than in the days before Eliza came to them. He knew he needed to help

Tommy, Enrique, and Durwood Todd more, but he just could not get enough of his baby daughter. *His daughter*. Those words were still foreign to him, but he liked them. They made him smile.

A change had come over Spring, although she could not see it in herself. Her smile and laugh came more readily, and the light in her eyes had returned. The sadness of the last couple of years had left with the coming of Eliza. She was once again the woman Hewey had married.

Eliza was thriving. Hewey had wondered if the milk from Walter's Jersey cow would suit her little body, but it seemed he had worried for nothing. She was growing, and like her parents, was very happy.

One evening in early summer, Hewey and Spring sat on the front porch of their rock house, Eliza sleeping in Spring's lap. The evening breeze was pleasant there in the shade. Far to the east, rain clouds had built. They could smell the rain, the most optimistic smell in West Texas. The clouds appeared to be moving away, but no matter where they were headed, evening rain clouds were always pleasant to watch in the desert country.

Hewey took it all in, thinking about the path his life had taken recently. So much had changed in under a year. He had spent much of his life wandering, refusing every attempt or nudge by family and friends to settle in one place. There had always been something better or more interesting over the next hill.

Ownership of anything more than a good horse or two would have been a burden, he had thought back then. If he could not pack something on a horse, then he had not wanted to own it.

He looked across the ranch, *his ranch*, and then over at Spring and Eliza. Spring did not notice his stare; she was too focused on her sleeping baby.

"You know," said Hewey finally. "At first I didn't even want this ranch. I just didn't like the idea of someone just givin' me something. I guess you know that."

Spring looked up at him. "I do."

"After a while I sort of decided it was all right, since I had given them somethin' way back then. I decided maybe it was okay for them to bless us if they wanted to."

Spring watched quietly as Hewey paused, composing his thoughts and perhaps also getting his emotions under control, at least enough to speak. It took nearly a full minute. "Now I think I still had it wrong. The Hendersons givin' us this place changed everythin' for us. There ain't no doubt about that."

A single tear fell down Hewey's cheek, and he let it fall. "But that little girl right there," he said, pointing at the sleeping Eliza. "That's the blessing."

John Bradshaw

About The Authors

JOHN BRADSHAW is a West Texas native and award-winning journalist who has written for the San Angelo-based *Livestock Weekly* for twenty years. He is an avid horseman and a livestock producer. He lives outside the small town of Abernathy with his wife, Sara. His first novel, *Elmer Kelton's The Familiar Stranger*, was co-written with his friend, the late Steve Kelton.

ELMER KELTON (1926-2009) was the seven-time Spur Award-winning author of more than forty novels, including the Texas Rangers series, the Hewey Calloway series, and the Buckalew Family series. He was also the recipient of the Owen Wister Lifetime Achievement award. In addition to his novels, Kelton worked as an agricultural journalist for forty-two years, and he served in the infantry in World War II.